THAT OL' BLACK MAGIC

SILVER JAMES

THAT OL' BLACK MAGIC is a work of fiction. Names, characters, places, and incidents are either the product of the author's imagination or are used fictitiously, and any resemblance to actual persons living or dead is entirely coincidental.

THAT OL' BLACK MAGIC

Contact: silverjames@swbell.net

Cover design by *Clary Carey*, clarycarey@gmail.com
Cover Image: © Clary Carey

Edited by Gregory Alan

ISBN-13: 978-0-9899217-4-9
ISBN-10: 0989921743

Published in the United States of America
9 8 7 6 5 4 3 2 1

DEDICATION

To my dad, who gave me free rein to imagine, who instilled in me a
love of reading and books, and who was my best friend.
I miss you every day.

.

ACKNOWLEDGMENTS

When you tell people you're a writer, you can pay attention to the voices in your head—and talk back to them—and normal folks don't call you crazy. Usually. But when I'm under deadline and I forget to feed the fuzzy critters, and the two-legged ones, I'm thankful my family and friends understand I really am a little nutty during those times but it's okay.

I truly appreciate the help I receive from everyone—my critique partners, and cover artist, and my wonderful husband. Cheers to my beta readers who pointed out the flaws, laughed when they were supposed to, and appreciated the magicks'…erm…attributes.

Very special thanks go out to Kelly and Keiran. They were here at the beginning when Sade first entered the world of my imagination. They acted as my sounding board as I developed the world of Penumbra and the people who live there. A thank you to Justin for giving the series a name and one to a friend known simply as Traveller for lending a voice to a certain werewolf.

Last but definitely not least, I have to recognize my readers. Each email, Facebook comment, tweet, and visit to my website convinces me that maybe I can put a bunch of words together and tell a story. One last caveat: Any and all mistakes are my own.

CHAPTER ONE
DÉJÀ VU ALL OVER AGAIN

THIS WAS ONLY DAY ONE of what was shaping up to be a bloody weird week and the gods had been drinking again. Too bad Sade Marquis didn't have that option. She was on duty. Dammit. Not to mention it was only ten in the morning. However, if things got any stranger, she might change her mind.

She occupied the one booth that gave her a broad view of the whole place. Déjà Vu. All over again. Back in the early days, right after graduating from the FBI Academy, the New Orleans Field Office had been her first assignment. She'd leased an apartment upstairs from the Déjà Vu. The bar-restaurant combo became a second home. Open twenty-four/seven, she could eat no matter the time of day.

Jax Martine—or as she liked to think of him "a Jax of all trades"—sailed by her table and two glasses of ice water appeared in his wake. He was human, but Sade would bet dollars to donuts there was a witch in his family tree. She glanced at her watch and wondered if she could squeeze in a late breakfast. She was meeting her partner, who had no concept of time. Werewolves were like that.

Catching Jax's attention, Sade wiggled her fingers through a complicated series of gestures. A plate with eggs, bacon, and French toast—*real* French toast made from thick-cut slices of crusty French bread—appeared a few minutes later, along with two more glasses of ice water to replace the ones she'd drained.

She was on her third cup of post-breakfast coffee when two girls sitting at the bar stirred. Their attention swiveled to the front door, eyes on the prime specimen of fae male swaggering into the shadowed space. Back-lit by a sunshine nimbus, Ariel made quite an entrance. Sade looked to heaven for a reprieve that didn't come. Her day just kept getting better and better.

Ariel, known through every realm as the King's Seducer, did not appreciate being called to heel by a human. Not even this one. He'd done his best to occupy her bed for over ten years now—to no avail. Despite her rejections, his breath still hitched every time he saw her and he couldn't explain the reason. Perhaps that's why he kept coming back for more of the shit she handed out. As he slid into the booth opposite Sade, she arched a brow.

"Still having trouble keeping it up, Ari?"

His reflection shimmered in the glass covering a colorful poster hanging behind Sade's head. The points of his ears peeked through his tawny hair and his skin glimmered with a silvery sheen. Ariel ramped up his magic to keep the glamour in place.

Ariel's gaze flicked between his reflection and Sade. "I'm guessing you're not here because there are new ripples in the Veil."

Sade pursed her lips and forced back a laugh as Ariel's gaze tracked to her mouth as sure as a bird dog on point. He was so easy.

"That's a concern, yes." She dropped her voice. "Magicks are only now getting control back, Ari, and human vigilantes are still out there just looking for an excuse to go all Spanish Inquisition on your ass."

The lower half of his face quirked into something resembling a nonchalant smirk. "You'd like an excuse to check out my ass." When Sade didn't rise to his bait, he added, "Just mine or magicks in general?"

"Have you heard anything on the grapevine?" Sade refused to play his games. Not this morning. She had a noon date with Marie Laveau. Or at her tomb, anyway.

"You used to be fun, Sade. Before you got all uptight and started carrying a gun."

"I'll take that as a no. I'm outta here." She slid toward the end of the booth but Ari's hand on her arm stopped her.

"Not here."

"I am *not* going back to your hotel, Ari."

The breath he blew out was strong enough to ruffle the hair falling over his forehead. "Gods, Sade. Seriously? Do you really believe that's all I think about?"

The look she leveled his direction said it all. "Okay. I suppose I deserved that. A little. I would bed you in a heartbeat, Sade Marquis, and it has nothing to do with the King's mandate. But your heart belongs to another." He paused a beat. "How is the mutt anyway?"

Sade's lips pursed and Ari fought the tightening of his groin at the thought of those lips around his cock. The wench knew exactly what she did to him. Her eyes glittered as she tilted her head toward the entry.

"Why don't you ask him yourself?"

Caleb Jones didn't pause at the door to let his eyes adjust. A werewolf, his night vision was even better than a vampire's. Slightly over six feet tall, lean and wiry, he stalked across the room toward their booth. Sade scooted over and he slid into the space next to her. He glared at Ari. Ari glared back.

"Boys, this is neutral ground. No piss fights in here. Besides, we all know my dick is bigger."

"Geez, Sade. Watch your language." Caleb's long-suffering expression prompted her to add fuel.

"Shut the fu—" The end of that word was lost in a whoosh of breath as Caleb squeezed her thigh.

Ari smirked. "That'll leave a bruise." He studied the two people across from him. "You realize she does it just to yank your chain. Stop chastising her and she'll clean up her act."

"The hell I will. Shut up, Ari. You don't know a gawd—"

Caleb squeezed her thigh again and she clamped her jaw shut. Ari wondered not for the first time about the depth of the relationship between human and werewolf. The two acted more like siblings than lovers sometimes. It bothered him that she'd taken the werewolf for a lover instead of him, and he didn't believe it was all about his ego. To hide the direction of his thoughts, he shaped his features into the bored expression he wore at the fae court. "Now that the gang's all here, what's going on?"

"I have a meeting at noon."

"And I'm here to back you up for that but why is he here?" Caleb growled the question as a feral light flickered in the depths of his eyes.

Before Ariel could raise his flattened palm to his mouth, Sade had her booted heel jammed between his legs. "The next time you resort to faerie dust, Ariel, I'll castrate you."

Werewolves were allergic to faerie dust. Being on the receiving end of a face full left them trapped in their current form. Had Ari blown that crap into Caleb's face, the werewolf would be unable to change into wolf form until the effects wore off. Ari had used the trick often to trap Caleb in one form or the other when Sade was a girl. And she needed Caleb ready for action.

Ari pretended he wasn't a little turned on by Sade's aggressive display even though he knew she'd follow through on her threat—or at least try. He'd watched her grow up, observed her childhood as King Oberon and the master vampire, Mathias DeVries, used her as a pawn. Then, on the King's orders, he'd attempted to seduce her from the age of fifteen on. Between the werewolf guard dog and the gargoyle Sentinel, who'd decreed himself her protector, aided and abetted by the girl's own stubbornness, he'd failed. Every time he'd tried. Ah, well. What did that Scottish poet say, 'The best laid plans?' Through the years, his flirtation had become a game. A game he intended to win some day.

4

"No way in hell, Ari." Sade didn't resist the urge to roll her eyes. "Your thoughts are as plain as day. I'm not going to bed with you. Ever."

Caleb stiffened beside her and he barely swallowed the growl rumbling in his chest.

"Relax, Caleb. I'm still a virgin, thanks to you and Roman scaring off every potential boyfriend I might have had."

The werewolf closed his eyes briefly and inhaled, letting his breath out slowly in an attempt at patience. "TMI, Sade. You still haven't answered my question. Why is the fae here?"

Ignoring Ari, Sade turned to her partner. "I found out he was in town and he always has good sources. I'm hoping he'll nose around for us."

"I thought the wolf was the one with the keen sense of smell." Ari watched them closely. Sade still a virgin? An intriguing thought. Perhaps he needed to rethink her relationship with the werewolf.

"Shut up, Ari. God. I feel like I'm dealing with toddlers when you two are in the same room. Grow up and leave the testosterone at the door. Something has the magicks stirred up down here and the Bureau sent us down to find out what." Sade closed her eyes and rolled her head on her neck in an attempt to ease the tension in her muscles.

Leaning her arms on the table, she lowered her voice. The two magicks would have no trouble hearing her but any human in the place would be unable to do so. "New Orleans has always been a haven. Neutral ground. From the beginning. Harmony between the magicks is only as good as last week's treaty but here? Here it really is *laissez les bons temps rouler.*"

"Yeah, let the good times roll. Along with some heads." Caleb's bitterness flavored his words.

"Ease off, Caleb. Every magick race has been losing people. That's why we're here. To find out why. The only confirmed DOA we have is the werewolf."

Ari straightened. "This is the first I've heard of that. By beheading? Who?"

Caleb's eyes flashed again but he managed to snarl out, "Victoria Smith."

"First daughter of the Smith clan?"

"Duh."

Ariel stared at Caleb, hoping he'd heard wrong. "Well...shit."

"Has already hit the fan, glitter boy."

Sade sat back, studying Ariel, while keeping a watch on Caleb with quick glances. The fae truly was shocked by the news and an emotion flickered across his face so quickly she couldn't identify it before his well-practiced mask shuttered his expression. Regret? Remorse? Or was that grief she saw in his eyes?

"I knew her. I am sorry, Caleb."

She openly watched the two now, amazed at the understanding passing between them. Holy shit. They'd both slept with the woman. And remembered her with fondness. Sade bit back a snarky retort. Victoria had affected them. Deeply. She sensed their grief and it made her wonder what it would feel like to be remembered with such affection.

Clearing her throat, Sade steered them back to the problem at hand. "She was here on vacation. When she didn't return to the hotel after a shopping trip, the Smith clan entourage went looking for her."

"Where was she found?" Ari's voice cracked.

Sade answered, "Along the Mississippi River near Chalmette. At the battlefield and national cemetery by a group of Boy Scouts picking up trash."

"What happened to her?"

"There was enough silver in her bloodstream to take down a pack of wolves." Caleb gritted out the words.

"Whoever took her knew she was a werewolf." Sade studied the men, noting their differences.

Ariel looked like a runner—all leg and long, lean muscles. Sun-kissed and tawny—hair and skin both. His hair always reminded her of a fawn's coat. His skin held a shimmer that was also apparent in silvery green eyes the color of high-grade jade.

Caleb was slightly taller, also lean, but broader, his muscles like coiled rope. His thick, dark brown hair hung in his eyes no matter how often he cut it and a dark five o'clock shadow defined his jaw unless he'd just shaved. Hair a shade darker formed a light thatch across his chest and abdomen where, in comparison, fine hair feathered across Ari's body. Caleb's eyes were the color of melted fudge but they glistened in the light and she often caught the flecks of feral red in their depths.

Humans would look at Ariel and wonder what was different about him. They'd look at Caleb and simply see a man—although not one to pick a fight with. How would a human know Victoria was a magick? More important, how would they know the way to weaken her enough they could take her head? A shiver skittered up her back and she refused to acknowledge the old wives' tale about walking over graves.

Ariel caught her gaze, held it for a long moment. "I'll ask around. We *will* find who did this."

Sade waited for a cymbal to clang or trumpets, bells, or…something. Ari's words felt weighted, like a vow, like something momentous should happen because he uttered them.

Her phone vibrated in her jacket pocket. "Crap." Jerking it out, she read the text. "Double crap." She glanced at Caleb. "We have to go."

He slid out of the booth and tossed down money for her breakfast before she could. "You can get my tab next time," Caleb said, cutting off her protest.

"I'll contact you when I have news, Sade." Ari's gaze slid away from hers and collided with Caleb's.

The two men shared a moment of understanding that left Sade looking in from the outside. She tried not to get pissed. Since she pretty much stayed that way, it was easier said than done.

Caleb followed her out into the muted morning light of the French Quarter. "What's up?"

"We have another one."

He tensed. "Wolf?"

Sade pulled him across the street and they walked half a block before she replied. "No. Fae."

CHAPTER TWO
GARDEN OF THE DEAD

THE BODY, LIKE A MACABRE art exhibit, hung splayed along the wrought-iron fence. Spiked finials penetrated the fae's chest. Even in death, he conveyed his otherworldly magnificence. Sade knew him. Sort of. He'd been a guard in Queen Titania's household. Alvin. She'd teased him, comparing him to the chipmunk. He'd hated her guts.

"Fuck." When Caleb didn't call her on the curse, Sade knew things were bad.

"Call Ariel. He'll need to notify the Court."

"I can't."

Caleb stared at her. "What do you mean you can't?"

"He can't be involved."

"The decedent is a fae, Sade. Ariel is a high-ranking member of the Court and therefore their representative."

"I know what the fuck he is, Caleb. And the protocol." She whirled on her best friend, her anger barely under control. "*I* have to be the one to notify Titania."

Caleb stared at her, his anger a match for hers. It was bad enough Ariel was in town but then to learn that he'd known Victoria, had slept with her, cared about her? He turned away, fought to get control of his emotions. Once upon a time, Deacon Smith, Victoria's father, and Romulus Jones, his alpha, had negotiated a mating between him and Tori.

Immature and selfish, they'd defied tradition. Ran off, had a brief affair, and then called it quits. Tori had been wild back then. He wasn't surprised she'd fallen for the King's Seducer.

But she'd matured, grown. And she'd been in New Orleans for one last fling before settling down with her mate.

Ignoring the urge to hunt and blood whoever had murdered Tori, Sade's words sunk in. "What do you mean *you'll* have to notify the Queen?"

The local cops looked way too interested in their conversation. Sade snagged his jacket and yanked him several paces away. "Alvin and Ariel. The Court can't know Ari is here in New Orleans."

"Why?"

"They have—*had* a blood feud."

Caleb rocked back on his heels. Within the magick realms, it didn't matter what flavor you were. A blood feud crossed all boundaries. But what concerned him most was that this was the first he'd heard of it. "They'll think he did it."

"Yes." She glanced back at the scene. "Make sure the locals don't touch anything. We need pictures but they aren't to touch the body. Fuckin' politics." She wanted to slam her head against the nearest wall—which happened to be Marie Laveau's tomb. On second thought, that probably wasn't a good idea. Not smart to piss off New Orleans' premier voodoo queen—alive *or* dead.

Her next problem was in contacting Ariel. Under normal circumstances, she thought about him and he showed up— especially when she didn't want him around. Of all the magick races, fae had the most trouble with modern technology. Cold iron was the bane of their existence and even with gold, silver, or copper components, cell phones were an iffy proposition. 'Can you hear me now?' took on a whole new meaning with the fae.

Sade glanced around the cemetery. With all the activity, the person she'd hoped to meet wouldn't be caught dead within miles of the place. Unless...

"Any chance your informant did this?"

She glanced at Caleb. "I was just wondering the same thing. But it's daylight and tourists are in and out of here all the time. My guy is shifty—" She cut her eyes toward the werewolf. "No pun intended. He's slick but violence isn't his thing." She leaned in closer. "See a raven anywhere?"

"Bwarck-arck-arck."

Looking up, she glared at the raven perched on the top of the nearest tomb. "No need to make fun of me." Ravens weren't the most reliable messengers in the preternatural world but sending one beat trying to reach Ariel by cell phone. And they could be bought cheap with anything shiny.

The glossy bird opened its beak but closed it as Sade made a shut-it motion with her fingers. She pulled a short string of shiny beads from her pocket. "Find Ariel. Tell him to get out of town now. And to call me when he has the chance."

The raven bobbed its head, stretching toward Sade. She held the string up and the bird grasped the beads in its beak then launched into the sky. Turning back to the crime scene, Sade jammed her hands in her pockets and sighed deeply. "I so do not want to talk to the Queen."

"Why do you have to call Titania? Why not Oberon?"

"Because Alvin was one of hers."

"Then call her social secretary."

Sade opened her mouth to reply. Closed it. Opened. Closed. And added a few blinks for good measure. "That's freaking brilliant!" Due to that whole technologically challenged thing, the fae court relied on human employees. She wouldn't have to speak to Titania at all.

Ten minutes later, with a call to Las Vegas and Titania's human secretary made, Sade only needed to subdue the locals while explaining representatives from the fae court would arrive to retrieve Alvin's body and that she was taking over the investigation.

"Look, I know how you feel, detective. Trust me, I'd rather be anywhere but here and I wish like hell there wasn't a dead fae courtier hanging on the fence."

The NOPD homicide cop looked like a bad caricature—jowly face, sweat-stained armpits, and a paunch hiding both his belt buckle and his holster. At least he didn't have the stub of a cigar jammed in the corner of his mouth. "Look, cher—" He swallowed what he was about to say as five warriors in full court dress arrived in a cloud of faerie dust.

Caleb immediately retreated behind the nearest crypt, leaving Sade to face them on her own.

"Agent Marquis." The oldest offered the barest incline of his head in acknowledgment. Anyone else would have felt slighted.

"Baron Korred. I didn't expect you to come yourself."

The fae's expression altered as he stared past Sade's shoulder. A flicker of anger disturbed the boredom inherent in the fae's countenance. "This was not an accident."

The four warriors accompanying Korred moved as one to Alvin's body. They gently extracted him from the fence, careful not to touch the wrought iron. None of the humans moved. They looked dumbstruck. Or bespelled. It was sometimes hard to tell the difference. Fae *au natural* had that effect on mundanes. Sade watched as they laid Alvin on a cloak and wrapped his body in its golden folds.

"What are you not telling me, Agent Marquis?"

Sade stewed over what to say, and more important, how to couch the words. Dealing with the fae court was treacherous at best and deadly at worst.

The baron didn't give her long to think. "Where is Ariel?"

Well, hell. That cat got out of the bag quickly. She could at least answer Korred's question honestly. "I don't know."

"You are aware of the blood feud?"

"I am aware there is...*was* one. But Ariel was with me when this occurred."

"You are certain of that?"

"I am."

"You understand the consequences of such a voucher?"

Sade did her best not to gulp. "There are human witnesses. And my partner. Ariel was already with me when Caleb arrived."

The baron made a strangled noise and she glanced at him. His expression twisted into one of disgust. "We do not accept—"

She snarled and cut him off. "Do not finish that sentence, Baron. You forget who I am. Who he is. This is a whole new world and the lines between the magicks are no longer valid." He opened his mouth but her raised index finger stopped him. "Don't. This is the only warning you will get from me. I know damn well what you are thinking. Ariel did not do this. And Caleb is a finer man than any ten fae I've met in my lifetime."

The fae attempted to look superior. "You have lived a short life."

"And met way too many douche bag fae since Oberon snatched me from my cradle."

He *tsked* at her. Sade bit her tongue and counted to ten to control her temper. She hated it when a magick freaking *tsked* at her like she was some recalcitrant child.

"This is the way it works, Korred." She intentionally ignored his title. "Under the new laws, I didn't have to contact you. I didn't have to offer the ceremony to Alvin. But I did. I *know* how important it is to your kind. I've trampled all over human law to ensure his return to the Summerlands. I've probably compromised my investigation. But fuck it. What's the death of one magick in the scheme of things, right?"

Korred watched her from half-lowered lids. "Do you know the origin of the blood feud?"

"Don't know, don't care."

"You should, human. You should care very much."

"What the hell does that mean? Are you threatening me?"

"No. But you should learn about the fae who hides behind you."

"Ariel? Hiding behind me? Not hardly."

"Do not be so quick to make claims about something of which you know nothing." Korred watched as the four warriors gathered Alvin's body. "We will avenge him."

"The hell you say." Sade stood toe-to-toe with the fae. "I am the law here. Not you. Not Oberon. Not Titania. Not the fucking magick council. Me. Now get out of my sight before I arrest you, throw everyone in a cage of cold iron, and send Alvin for a human autopsy."

"You would not dare."

"Try me, buster. Now get out of my face. You're breathing my air and I wouldn't want to contaminate your perfect fae genetics with my tainted human ones."

One moment the fae were there and the next they were gone. The humans breathed—one collective breath inhaled and exhaled before returning to normal. Caleb waited for the dust to settle before he approached.

"Buster? You called the fae ankou *buster?*" He sat on a nearby tomb, his breath wheezing as he laughed.

The NOPD detective stared at her with something akin to awe on his face. "Damn, cher. You might be insane but you got guts." He watched Caleb and fought the grin forming on his own face. "What be this *ankou* thing though?"

Sade glared at Caleb as she answered, "Ankous are the grim reapers of the magical realm. They accompany a dead magick on their final journey."

"You be careful, cher. That thing might come lookin' for you some dark night."

"He's right, Sade."

She jumped almost a foot off the ground, whirling in midair to face the fae who'd appeared silently behind her. "Gawddammit, Ari. You aren't supposed to be here."

"You did something very stupid today, Sade. You made an enemy of the Baron."

Snorting, Sade rolled her eyes. "So what else is new? He's hated my guts since I was two and tossed my cookies on his favorite boots."

Ari leaned his shoulder against the peeling white paint of the voodoo queen's crypt and did his best to look nonchalant—a task not easy to do under Sade's withering glower.

"We need to talk." Caleb stopped laughing and sat up. Ari could almost see the werewolf's ears prick forward in interest. "Just you and me, Sade."

She crossed her arms over her chest, chin jutting. Stubbornness oozed from every pore of her body. And he wanted her. As he always had. The shy girl with pudgy cheeks and flyaway hair had melted into this sleek, fearless woman. Too fearless. Ari glanced at Caleb. The werewolf was on his feet, alert, watchful.

"It's important."

CHAPTER THREE
BLOOD FEUD

SADE STARED AT ARIEL. He looked downright serious—something new where the fae was concerned. If asked for one word to describe him, she would have pulled "frivolous" out of the air. Wine, women, and roguery. She had a third "w" word in mind but she doubted that wanker or wanking actually applied to Ari. Women lined up around the block to be with the King's Seducer and from what she heard through the magical grapevine, he left them fulfilled and wanting more.

"I see the wheels turning, Sade."

Was that resignation in his voice? Caleb started to speak but Sade shut him up with a look. "Go soothe the ruffled natives, Caleb. Okay?" At her partner's nod, she gestured for Ari to follow as she strolled toward the front of the cemetery and the gate leading to the busy street on the other side of the wall. A knot of people gathered on the sidewalk waiting to tour the historic crypts, but kept out by two uniformed officers and flapping yellow crime scene tape.

Slipping past, Sade headed down the block with Ariel close on her heels. She rounded the corner and stopped, giving the fae an opportunity to grab her around the waist. His hands lingered until she cleared her throat. Sade stepped away and leaned against the whitewashed stucco and brick wall surrounding the cemetery.

Ariel studied her expression, his eyes taking in all the nuances. "You should be more careful, Sade."

"Why? Because I shouldn't piss off some high fae fuckity-fuck?"

"Yes."

"Aren't you some high fae fuckity-fuck?" She arched a brow provocatively.

"I am, yes."

"Don't I piss you off regularly?"

He resisted the urge to sigh. The woman drove him to distraction. "I'm serious, Sade."

"You? Serious? Give me a break."

Barely suppressing the urge to shake her, Ari turned his back to her and breathed deeply.

"See?" She couldn't resist the tease.

"Please, Sade."

Something in the tone of his voice alerted Sade to the gravity of the situation. "Okay. I'm listening, Ariel."

"You have enemies in the fae realm, Sade."

"Oh, duh! So tell me something I don't know."

"Just listen for a change, Child."

Sade's temper spiraled but she bit back her retort. She belatedly caught the emphasis he'd placed on the word "child." The way he said it, it was like a title rather than a dig about her human youth compared to the ancient age of the fae. She waited.

"I don't need to give you a play-by-play of your childhood. Nor must I remind you of how we met." He turned to watch her and when she didn't retort as he expected, he continued. "Yes, King Oberon ordered me to seduce you, to take the virginity humans seem to value so highly from you." Sex, even in the magical world, was a complicated matter though the act didn't hold the same stigma humans placed upon it. Sex was enjoyable. Or a weapon. A reward. Sex was many things to magicks and virginity was a state best shed early. "While it became a game between us, Titania was far more serious."

Sade furrowed her brow. "I don't understand."

17

"No, you don't." He raised his hand to stay her rebuttal. "I never wanted you to understand. Titania sent Alvin to accomplish what I had not. Roman, as your bodyguard, would have killed him because Alvin would not have been deterred. I could not have the gargoyle compromised. He needed to be at your side."

"Compromised? What do you mean *compromised?*"

"Roman was acting as an official envoy at the time, Sade. He's a Sentinel. Had he killed Alvin, there would have been…consequences. Repercussions that would have reached deep into the realms." His gaze slid away from hers. Sometimes, she was far too smart for her own good.

Sade watched him, noted when he refused to meet her eyes, and waited until she was sure her voice would be steady before she asked, "What did you do, Ariel?"

He stared off, watching the traffic whooshing by but not really seeing it. "I did what was necessary, Sade. To keep you safe. Alvin's orders were to seduce you or kill you. I would not let either happen."

"Well hell, Ariel."

"Indeed."

"You aren't going to tell me, are you?"

"What occurred between Alvin and me need not—"

"Shut up, Ari." She grabbed his arm and moved in front of him so he would have to look at her. "It does concern me. You risked a blood feud for me. And now you're under suspicion because Alvin was stupid enough to get killed in the same city where you happen to be."

He schooled his features into one of studied nonchalance but she saw right through it. "Dammit, dammit, dammit, fuck it all to hell." She wanted to shake him. "Has he been gunning for you all this time?"

"No."

That surprised the hell out of her. "Alvin never impressed me as the kind of guy who'd walk away from a personal fight."

"He had no choice."

"He had no choice, or you didn't give him one?"

"Both."

Sade swallowed the urge to yell. "You really need to talk to me, Ari."

A series of honking horns and yells from vehicles passing by caught Ariel's attention and he moved back from the curb. With the wall at his back, he stared at the sidewalk as if he could read his fortune in its cracks. "Some things are not meant to be shared with mundanes, Sade. Suffice it to say that had I revealed what I knew, Alvin would have faced a sentence of death."

"Whoa. Wait just a minute. You had evidence that this dude was guilty of crimes so serious the fuckin' fae court would have put him death? And you didn't do anything about it?" Sade slugged his arm, not that he really felt it.

"I did what I had to do, Sade."

"To keep me safe? Right? That's your excuse?" She pivoted on her heel and stormed away. After ten feet, she whirled and marched back.

Her hands were clenched into fists and her bottle green eyes glinted like broken glass under the noonday sun. It was all Ari could do to keep from reaching for her. He loved seeing her angry, with those flashing eyes and heightened color. She was so full of...humanity when she was like this. Alive and real and he wanted her with an aching so divine it took his breath away.

The growl behind him raised the hair on the back of his neck. Caleb. The damn wolf was never far from her side. He couldn't retreat, caught as he was between the two of them.

"Sade, that homicide detective wants to talk to you." Caleb didn't give her a chance to argue. "Now."

She read something in his expression that had her detouring around Ariel and striding around the corner headed back to the cemetery's front gate.

"Back off, Jones."

"The hell I will, you glittering sonavabitch."

Ariel almost laughed. For the first time that he could remember, Caleb Jones sounded as crude as most of his brethren. The werewolf had been raised with Sade in the house of Mathias DeVries, master vampire and head of the vampire council. Sade had the foul mouth and wretched manners. Caleb worked hard to keep his animal side at bay.

"Jealous?" Ariel arched a brow to punctuate the superior smirk splashed on his face.

"Of you?" Caleb's laughter exploded in a harsh bark. "Not hardly."

"Fair notice, wolf. I will win her."

Caleb rolled his eyes. "Yeah, good luck with that."

"Do you believe she loves you so much?"

"I know she does. But see? Here's the difference, fae. I love her back. You aren't capable of loving anyone but yourself."

"She's still a virgin."

"And your point is?"

"Why have you not bedded her, Jones?"

"Why have you been so convinced I had all these years?" Caleb grinned, his lips stretching enough to flash his canines. "I could smell your jealousy this morning, Ariel. You reeked of it." He tilted his face skyward, sniffed, and smirked. "Still do."

"You have shared her bed."

"Yep. Sure have. Enjoyed every minute of it."

Ariel's hands curled and uncurled, the gesture an unconscious indication of his inner turmoil. He forced his face to smooth into a bland expression. Caleb baited him. Nothing more.

"And yet you have not...how would your kind put it? Fucked her."

"And what would you fuckin' fae call it, Ariel? Would you *make love* to her? Is that what your seduction was all about? She was fifteen when you first showed up. She didn't even have a driver's license yet. Wasn't legal by mundane standards. She's not like us. She's human, Ariel. Why can't you get that through all the damn glitter you call a brain? You only showed up because the goddamned king ordered you to stick your dick in her pussy."

Ariel bristled. "And so you show your true colors, wolf. That's what you would do to her. You would take her like the animal you are."

Caleb shook his head, the expression in his eyes reflecting sadness. "And that's what you just don't get about them, Ariel. What you will never understand. It's all about the sex for you. Humans are all about feelings. And until you figure that out, you'll never have a chance with Sade." He rolled his head on his neck. "Look, believe it or not, I didn't come out here to fight with you. If you have something on Alvin, I need to know."

"What I had on Alvin has nothing to do with his death."

"How can you be so sure?"

"Because Victoria is also dead. I do not believe the two events are random." Ariel watched Caleb, assessing the other man. "Why did you not mate with Victoria?"

"She didn't love me. And she wasn't ready to be faithful." Caleb tossed off his answer with the negligent lift of one shoulder.

"That's true then? That when a werewolf takes a mate, they remain faithful?"

Caleb's snort of laughter disturbed the flock of pigeons that had settled on the top of the wall. "No. It's only the female who has to remain faithful. To make sure the pup has the correct father. It sucks, but that's the rule."

"There are many things about your culture I will never understand."

"Ha, don't feel like the Lone Ranger, *kemosabe*."

Ariel stared at him completely lost. "Let me guess, that's some sort of pop reference."

Rolling his eyes, Caleb turned to walk away. "Something like that. We're at the Holiday Inn Chateau LeMoyne just down the block from Déjà Vu. Check in if you find out anything about Tori."

"Did you love her?"

Caleb stiffened but didn't turn around. "No. But I cared about her. I want whoever did this to her."

Ariel watched as Caleb continued to walk away. "For human justice? Or magick?"

The werewolf stopped and turned. "Now that's the question, isn't it?"

CHAPTER FOUR
STILL OF THE NIGHT

THE GREEN, SOUR APPLETINI SPLATTERED across the sleeve of Sade's leather jacket. Her favorite leather jacket. The woman next to her at the bar appeared clueless. And drunk. Not a good combination. Of course, the liquid grace of the hunk strolling Sade's direction left every female in the place with spilled drinks. And damp panties.

Sade watched the man's approach through the mirror behind the bar. Ariel was better—and worse—than almonds dipped in dark chocolate served in brandy and poured over ice cream. The King's Seducer. Sade smirked at the title. She was his one great failure. Her conscience twinged just a bit. Ari *had* ignited a blood feud on her behalf but old habits died hard.

Fae politics. Uncle Obi-wan and Queen Tittyfae. King Oberon wanted her ruined, in that whole, puritanical sense. Ariel had tried. Often. Caleb, foster brother, best friend, and self-proclaimed champion of her virtue, bit him in the ass so Ari had failed in his first attempt. The damn fae wouldn't take no for an answer. He'd been trying to score ever since.

And now, she'd learned that Queen Titania had ordered her own hit on Sade. If she were honest, Sade would have to admit she owed Ari one—not that she'd ever tell him so.

"Hello, love." Ari stopped right behind her, his body not quite pressed against hers. His warm breath tickled the fine hairs on the back of her neck. Damn. Tonight would be the night she'd worn her hair up. "You look fetching as always."

That last line was delivered with a quirked eyebrow and a sniff. Ari slipped his arms around her waist as he sniffed again and frowned. "What is that odor?"

Sade stared pointedly at the buxom blonde next to her, the one still holding an empty martini glass and staring open-mouthed at Ariel. "Frou-frou drinks stink. What can I say?"

"How 'bout a kiss?" His smile appeared winsome in the mirror, though his eyes twinkled with mischief. She grabbed him by the short hairs through his designer jeans. Wincing, Ari glanced down, waggled his brows, and added, "To make it all better?" She squeezed harder. His voice squeaked. "Not even a little one?"

"Nope."

With a resigned sigh, he raised his hands in surrender. "You win."

She dropped her hand and winked. "I always do." She motioned for the bartender. "What're you drinking, Ari?"

He shook his head. "Nothing."

Staring at the fae through the mirror for a minute, Sade finally swiveled on her bar stool to face him. "What's up?"

"Care to take a walk?"

Something about his expression worried her. Sade placed a twenty dollar bill on the bar to cover her Diet Coke with a lime and a big tip. The blonde with the big hair and bigger boobs glared before sliding her gaze to Ari, at which point she puckered up and blew kisses his direction. Ari shuddered, which upped Sade's respect meter a notch.

The noise level on the street was a gentle balm to Sade's hearing. The Carousel Bar at the Hotel Monteleone was tame compared to the places on Bourbon Street, but walking along Royal Street, only the whoosh and occasional toot of horns from passing taxis broke the stillness.

Ari offered his hand and Sade felt compelled to take it—not from any glamour or magic he pulled on her, but simply because she'd never seen Ariel appear so out of place. He looked positively shocked when her fingers entwined with his and she started down the sidewalk in the general direction of the French Quarter.

"Leave your jacket with me. I'll have it cleaned."

Sade slowed her casual stroll to a dawdle, casting dubious glances toward the handsome fae at her side. "Are you running a fever?"

He let out an exasperated breath. "I can't do something nice for you?" He stopped and tugged on her hand. "Do you really think I'm such a total prick, Sade?"

Her mouth opened and closed several times and she looked desperate. Ari was almost sorry he'd pushed things. There was safety in their well-defined relationship if not affection. Not for the first time he cursed the king and queen for their interference. Ariel was the one who was desperate— longing to establish the same easy companionship Sade shared with Caleb and Roman.

How could he blame Sade for considering him an enemy after all the grief the fae court had heaped on her? Sade's mother, a Vegas show girl, had been Oberon's mistress when she seduced a mild-mannered CPA from Dallas in order to get pregnant. It was all part of her plan to trap the man she knew as Oliver King. A problem arose when Titania found out and it was discovered that William Marquis was in the employ of Mathias DeVries. Oberon and Mathias feuded for years, with Sade their unwitting pawn.

She'd been a solemn child, wide-eyed and intelligent. Aware of things most humans remained ignorant of, the human little girl accepted her place in the preternatural world with an aplomb most adults would fail to achieve. She'd grown into a beautiful, self-assured woman who turned heads everywhere. Sade hid her scars but he knew they were there, evidenced by her rebellious streak, the cussing, the anger. When had she gotten so angry? The emotion crackled just beneath her skin, tingeing it with faint traces of electricity.

Glancing away from Ariel's intensity, Sade watched people strolling on the other side of the street. When her gaze returned to his face, she offered up a small shrug. "I like rules, Ariel."

Laughter curled and danced inside him before escaping with ease. "Rules? You? If ever there was someone who lived to break them, I'd say it was you, Sade Marquis."

"Exactly. If I don't know the rules, then I can't break them, right?" She turned and walked forward, tugging him along with her. They were almost the same height and he always found that a bit disconcerting. Whenever they were facing, it would take so little to close the distance, to taste her lips, to discover the sweetness lingering there.

They walked like lovers through the scattered light sprinkled along their way by streetlamps. When they reached Jackson Square, the park was closed, gates padlocked for the night, but benches ringed the fence, beckoning couples into the shadows. Sade led him to an empty bench facing St. Louis Cathedral. A noisy group approached, led by a man with sweeping blond hair and wearing a black satin poet's shirt.

"The vampire tours aren't nearly as cool now that the tourists know they actually exist."

Ari chuckled but didn't speak while they waited for the tour group to disappear around the corner. If any of his peers saw him, he might be embarrassed but he didn't really care. It felt…nice. Sitting here like this, holding Sade's hand. No politics. No games, beyond the comfortable flirting they'd fallen into over the years.

He glanced at their entwined fingers. "Does this bother you?"

Sade leaned away from him, her gaze flicking over his face as she attempted to decipher his expression. "Am I supposed to be flattered?"

She didn't disappoint. Ever. And that was part of the problem. "Maybe."

"Ha!" She rolled her eyes but felt a little off balance. Ariel was never serious. Ever. If he wasn't trying to get into her pants he was angling for introductions to any cute females of her acquaintance. Since she didn't do the whole gal pal thing,

Ari usually focused on irritating her. She tugged on her hand but the fae tightened his grip around her fingers. Gently, as if he wasn't ready to let her go. "What's up with you?"

He leaned back against the bench, face toward the sky as he watched clouds shuttle across the half-moon. "Nothing."

"Bullshit. Dude, you fucking declared a blood feud because of me. Oh, and forgot to mention it."

She glowered at him, a look that would have withered a lesser magick. A mundane would have curled up in the fetal position and cried like a baby. He'd seen them do so. He returned his gaze to the kaleidoscope of light and shadow playing across the sky.

"And now you're all…solemn and shit. Don't tell me you're finally growing a conscience after a millennium or so."

Ari pasted an affronted look on his face and turned to her. "Never."

She opened her mouth to retort but snapped her jaws shut on whatever she'd meant to say. They sat apart but for their joined hands. Voices filtered through the night. Cars traveled a distant street and when the wind kicked up, music drifted in from Bourbon Street. Neither spoke, unwilling to break the stillness of the night. But neither felt particularly comfortable.

Something lurked just beyond the edge of senses—magick *and* mundane—like a dark shadow slipping over the earth. Ari tensed and Sade had her free hand on the pistol holstered at her waist.

"What the hell?" The words she whispered were not the lover's endearment he longed for.

"The Veil. It just ripped again."

"Fuck."

CHAPTER FIVE
SILVER LINING

SADE AND ARIEL JUMPED TO their feet as the ground rumbled beneath them. Pigeons roosting atop St. Louis Cathedral burst into the air, wings sounding like applause. Confused in the dark, the birds circled looking for safe haven. Sade stared at Ariel, weapon automatically in her hand as she searched for any threat.

A red haze obscured the moon and an oily stench burned Sade's nose each time she inhaled. The air stank of rotten eggs and ammonia, making her eyes water. A sound like leather gloves rubbing together whispered above her. She instinctively stepped in front of Ariel. Which was stupid. She was human. He was immortal fae.

Seven feet of magick landed and relief washed over her. Sade managed to remain rooted to the spot despite every instinct urging her to run to the gargoyle to be safely ensconced in his arms and sheltered by his wings.

Roman glared at Ariel, who glared back. Always with the glaring, these magical creatures in her life.

"No fighting, you two. Something bigger and badder is happening." Her cell phone chirped and she answered it, keeping a wary eye on the gargoyle and the fae. Their animosity was legendary but she didn't have time at the moment to worry about fae politics and gargoyle protective instincts.

"Director." She turned her back on the two as she greeted George Bailey, the FBI Director and her boss.

"What the hell just happened, Marquis?" His gruff voice grated her eardrum. "That had to be magical because there's no way a world-wide earthquake could happen."

"No clue, sir. I'm sending out inquiries now." She peered at Roman and Ari, waggled her brows and shot a questioning look their way. They glanced at each other, gazed back at her, and shrugged. If they didn't know, she had no chance of figuring it out on the spot. "Let me do some digging. I'll get back to you."

"Sooner, not later, Marquis."

"Yessir." She hung up and stared at the two magicks. "So? What the hell just happened?" She held up a finger. "That was a direct fucking quote from the director of the FBI. Do not lecture me on cussing."

Ariel and Roman exchanged amused glances. They weren't quite as hard on her communication skills as Caleb was.

"Something disturbed the Veil." Roman's voice sounded like tires on a gravel road.

"Well, duh. Even I could figure that out, Roman. I want to know what that *something* is." She glared at Ariel.

"Don't look at me. I'll return to the court to see if they have any news."

"Let me know ASAP, Ari." She glanced up at the red moon. "That's freaking me the hell out."

The two magicks once again exchanged glances and Sade frowned. "What?" Neither spoke. "Fine. Ariel, get your butt back to Glitterland. Find out what King Obi-wan has to say." He disappeared in a spray of faerie dust as she turned to Roman. "Why are you here?"

"Glad to see you, too, Lady Sade."

The childhood nickname liquefied her insides. She stepped into Roman's embrace, her arms sliding around his waist as she rested her cheek against his chest. "I didn't expect to see you this trip, Romo." She fell into use of her own nickname for the gargoyle.

"I'm never far way, little one."

Sade blinked hard, swearing it was the foul air making her eyes tear up. "You realize you are the only being in the universe who gets to call me that, right?"

"And I am honored to do so. I came because something is stirring. Something ancient and evil but I cannot discover what or where."

"Crap. That doesn't bode well."

"No. It does not. I have discussed this with Mathias at the behest of *Le Viele*. Then I discovered you'd been sent here. There are things afoot that also do not bode well. For humans or the Realms."

"Damn. If the Old One is riled up, things can't be good." She worried her bottom lip between her teeth. "I still have nightmares about the months following the Big Rip."

Roman's chiseled features reverted to the solemn expression he usually wore. "Those were bad times, Sade. Violence spilling between the planes and too much blood. The *Concilium Magicae* was hard pressed to maintain the Accords. The peace among the Realms and humans is still tenuous. Your human scientists' explanation made little sense, especially with the continuing disturbances."

"Wait. I thought the Council came up with that whole celestial event tale. That wild star astronomers called The Flyer aligning with Mars during a lunar eclipse? Seriously? It never made sense to me. And then the solar eclipse two weeks later ripping the Veil the rest of the way?"

A troubled expression crossed Roman's face. "No one understands what caused the Veil to rip, Sade. But we all must deal with the aftermath. Three years is the blink of an eye in the whole scheme of things.

"Well, I guess if there's a silver lining to any of this, it's that you're here, Roman. I've missed you." She exhaled, and pretended it wasn't a sigh. "Can you stay awhile? So we can talk? But not here. That smell is gross."

At his nod, she led him around the corner of the park toward the river. The odor of the mules and manure along Canal Street was almost refreshing considering the hellish stench still clinging in her nostrils. They trudged—well, Sade did anyway—up the slope of the levee, crossed the railroad tracks and gained access to the walkway ribboning along the levee's top. To their right, lights from the Crescent City Bridge twinkled in the dark.

Sade took Roman's arm as they strolled but she didn't speak. A cool breeze danced across the river to play tag with her hair and she shivered at the sensation of icy fingers. Roman was content to remain quietly by her side even when she stopped to stare out across the water. When she shivered again, with no wind to tease her, he broke the silence.

"Is something wrong, Lady Sade?"

"Only with me, Roman."

"*Pfft.*"

She stiffened and turned an incredulous gaze his direction. "Did you just *pfft* me?" How big a train wreck had her life become when a freaking gargoyle *pffted* her? Sade turned and marched toward an empty bench. She sank onto it, eyes still searching the dark waters.

Roman settled beside her. "There is nothing wrong with you."

"Yes there is."

"Why do you believe so?"

Despite channeling her inner brat, Sade suddenly felt twelve again—all dressed up for her birthday party. The one no one attended despite a hundred invitations sent out.

When she didn't answer, Roman growled, the sound like rocks tumbling around in a tin can. "Is the fae bothering you again?"

Laughing, she cut her eyes to the man who had been both friend and protector. "Always. But that's just Ariel." Just Ariel. The King's Seducer. She'd learned it was an actual official title in the fae court. Ariel loved women. *All* women. Which, if Sade were truthful, was the whole problem. If she gave into his obvious charms then she would be just one of many. Okay, hundreds.

"How old is Ariel anyway?"

Roman offered her a bemused look.

Okay, make that thousands—or hundreds of thousands.

"What is this about, Sade?"

"Nothing. Nothing at all."

He arched a knowing brow. "Lady Sade?" His tone both wheedled and insisted she answer.

Leaning her elbows on her knees, she plopped her chin into her left palm. "It's stupid, Romo."

Roman schooled his expression. Sade was troubled—troubled deeply. He waited with the patience inherent to his kind, with the tolerance and forbearance that ensured his race's place as diplomats and peacekeepers. That gargoyles were all but impossible to kill and had memories lasting longer than history carved in granite also helped.

Sade sighed, a long indrawn gulp of air followed by an exasperated exhale. "It's stupid."

"You have expressed that sentiment already." He touched her chin with a gentle finger, lifting it from her palm as he turned her to look at him. His heart contracted at what he saw in her eyes—need, longing, a sad wistfulness that robbed him of his breath.

"I just want to be special, Roman."

"You are."

Her lids drooped to shutter her eyes but her emotions shimmered along her skin like foxfire dancing in the swamp.

"No. I'm not." She sounded small, not like herself at all. "Just once, Romo. Just once in my life I'd like to be special to someone. Just me."

Roman cupped her cheek but she leaned away from him. Opening her eyelids, she stared at the river once more. The lights from the bridge reflected in her eyes, sparking green flickers like moonlight on emeralds.

"The only man who's ever wanted to share my bed—"

He gripped her shoulders, twirling her to face him. "Stop." Roman barked the command and winced inwardly at the wave of hurt crossing her face. He gentled his voice. "Ahhh, Lady Sade. Have I always been honest with you?" She

32

nodded, her eyes fixed on his. "Then listen to my words, child. Many men will want you. They will flatter. They will cajole. They will promise and pledge. They will seduce. They want what you represent. What they think you can give them." A smile quirked the corner of his mouth and lit his dark gray eyes. "But for you, there will be only one man who needs. Who needs *you*. Only one whose heart beats solely for you. Keep your heart safe until the right one comes along."

Roman slid his palms along her arms and clasped both of her hands in his massive ones. "Will you do this? Not for me, but for yourself? Will you make this promise?"

Sade stared up at him. His expression remained gentle and solemn. She saw no pity there. Only true belief in what he said. "I promise."

The mournful echo of a tugboat's horn drifted across the water, riding on the heavy mist rolling in. The two of them sat, Sade tucked under Roman's arm, leaning against him. Mistaken for lovers by those who passed through the fog, they absorbed the night in companionable silence until the shrill ping of Sade's phone broke the silence.

"Fuck. We have another dead body."

CHAPTER SIX
SIGNS

SADE STARED DOWN AT THE burned husk as an ATF investigator appeared at her elbow.

"Didn't figure this to be an FBI case, Agent Marquis."

Inter-agency piss fights. Sade hated them. She checked the guy's sleeve for a patch. He was a bomb and arson tech—BATman. "I didn't either, until the big boss called and told me to get my ass out to this sorry piece of swamp."

A commotion at the door stopped the ATF agent from commenting. Sade didn't even turn around. "He's with me," she yelled over her shoulder.

Moments later, the guy jerked back. Seven feet of gargoyle had a tendency to scare the bejeesus out of a human, even if said human didn't know exactly what Roman was.

"Sade." The concern in Roman's voice was unmistakable.

"Roman." Sade didn't know what to say beyond his name.

"This is the third one."

"In three days." This was so not good. She exchanged a meaningful look with him.

"There will be repercussions."

"There already are." Oh, boy was there. Sade wondered for a moment if she should seriously reconsider her career choice. Getting confirmation from Roman about the seriousness of the situation didn't help.

The guy from ATF stared at one and then the other, working his mouth like a fish blowing bubbles but no words came out.

"Caleb is still checking the perimeter." Her werewolf partner had been running wild when the call came in. She'd grabbed clothes for him on the way to the scene and had also explained to Roman about the other deaths. Back in human form, Caleb now prowled around looking for scents. Werewolves had advanced lupine scenting abilities—obviously—but they were also adept at sniffing out magic, a skill mundane canines didn't have. And to kill a vampire at night would take magic. Lots of it.

Three dead magicks. In as many days. Magicks the humans knew nothing about until the Veil ripped. Magicks Sade sometimes wished she knew nothing about.

"We need to talk." Roman's voice echoed in the cavernous room.

"No shit, Sherlock." She resisted the urge to nudge the incinerated lump at her feet with her toe. Vampire ash played hell on leather boots and hers were new.

Sade pivoted and strode toward the roll-up doors of the warehouse, Roman right beside her.

"Yo, Feeb. You done here?"

She didn't break stride as she glanced over her shoulder. "Knock yourself out, Batman."

Outside, she leaned up against the ATF pickup parked in the weed-covered parking lot. The place had been abandoned for a few years. Any longer than that and the swamp would have completely reclaimed it.

"Are we headed back to the Dark Times, Roman?"

His unwavering gaze surveyed the area. "There are still pockets of humans resistant to the idea of our existence, Sade."

"Yeah." What could she say? When the Veil first ripped, there'd been blood running in the streets—human *and* magical. She'd heard stories of magical wars as a child. Hell, she'd been the trigger for a series of battles involving Mathias DeVries, master vampire and her godfather. Mathias gave *Master* whole new meaning. One of the oldest vampires in existence, he ruled the vampire Conclave with an unyielding fist. Pitted against him? Oberon, high king of the Seelie Court.

Magicks had always been entrenched in the human realm. Just no one thought to tell the mundanes about the magicks living masked by their glamours, gleefully enjoying life at the expense of humans. Then one day the Veil ripped. Bam. Humans woke up to discover there really were monsters under the bed and the things that went bump in the night were scarier than they'd ever imagined. That the president of the United States, Rhys Wynne, turned out to be an elf was both blessing and curse.

Legislation was quickly put into place to protect humans and magicks alike. Even so, retaliation on both sides had been brutal and deadly. Resentment continued to smolder. Fires occasionally flared up. Like now. That's why she and Caleb were here.

Her partner chose that moment to lope up. He offered a lopsided grin to Roman. "Heard you were in town, big guy. Come to help?"

The gargoyle's return smile appeared a little too enigmatic to suit Sade. She focused on her partner. "So? Anything?"

Caleb shook his head. His jaw was shadowed even though they were barely past the butt crack of dawn. Shaggy hair caressed his forehead and his brown eyes looked muddy in this light. "Nothing."

Sade furrowed her brow as she gazed around the scene. "What the hell?"

"Yeah, my thought, too. I figured we were dealing with a human. The silver, the cold iron, and now this. All overkill. But…"

"But. The vampire died last night and he wasn't staked." She tilted her head, studying the people on scene—the local ME's office, the ATF team, and the fire department. "He blazed high enough the building caught fire. That's what alerted the authorities."

Caleb shrugged. "Finding a skull with those incisors must have freaked them out."

"Especially since immolated vamps tend to turn straight to ash. No bones. No—" She blinked. "Caleb? Are you sure that's a vampire?"

The two magicks exchanged looks before returning their attention to her. "What are you thinking, Sade?" Caleb asked.

"Back before the Big Rip, there was a vampire subculture in some of the clubs here. A real vampire ran the scam, luring the kids in. Some of them had…dental work done." She stared at the open warehouse door, her lips pursed in speculation. "You got no scent of a spell?"

"None." Caleb's expression mirrored hers. "Nothing magical. No human smells beyond the first responders. Nothing. It's like all traces were wiped clean."

"That can't happen." Sade glanced up at Roman. "Can it?"

"Perhaps."

"What the hell does that mean?"

"Just what it says, Sade. There are ways to mask both scents."

"Agent Marquis?" A woman wearing a white contamination suit stood slouched in the door, halfway in the shadows. She shaded her hand over her eyes then straightened as she took in the two men standing with Sade.

"Jeez, you guys. Is there any woman immune to magick charms?" She strode across the lot to the woman.

"Just you, Sade," Caleb called after her.

"I'm Agent Marquis. What's up?" Sade pretended not to notice the disappointment on the woman's face.

"I won't know until I run further tests but I think your vampire was hit with acid."

"Acid?"

"Isn't that what I just said?"

"What kind?"

"What part of further tests did you not understand?"

Sade laughed. "I like you."

The assistant ME glared at her. "Whoopee. Remind me to pop the top on a cold beer when I get home to celebrate."

"Dr. Allison?" A voice from the interior interrupted.

"In a minute. I'm basking in the glory of my new fan club."

"Agent Sade Marquis."

"Dr. Toni Allison."

"A pleasure, Dr.—"

"Toni."

"Sade, And the beer's on me, Toni."

"Deal. As long as you bring those fine specimens of manhood with you."

"Figures. And here I thought you liked me for my sparkling personality."

"I've heard about you, Marquis. You don't sparkle. And neither did that vampire in there."

"So he *was* a vamp?"

"As opposed to what?"

"Human with a dental implant."

The doctor glanced over her shoulder. "Nope. I'm not an expert but I don't think human skin would have reacted the same way. The vic was vampire and he died screaming." She shuddered, a delicate motion Sade almost missed covered up as it was by the bio suit. "This is three."

"Yeah."

"What are we dealing with here, Marquis?"

"Wish I knew, Doc. Wish I knew." She pulled a card from her pocket and tucked it into the clipboard Toni held. "Call me when you get something."

"What are they?"

"S'cuse me?"

"Your friends. What are they?"

"Werewolf and gargoyle."

"Dayam."

"Yeah, they get that a lot. Call me, Doc."

"Absolutely."

Toni headed back inside the warehouse followed by Caleb and Roman. Sade laughed as the doctor tried to stall so the men would precede her. Oh, yeah, Toni wanted a look at their asses, and mighty fine butts they were. Her phone chimed with the theme to the Addams Family. Sade answered even though she knew who was likely on the other end.

"Marquis."

"You are in New Orleans. There is a dead scion."

Surprised, Sade sucked in a deep breath. She'd expected the caller to be Hoskins, the snooty butler employed by her godfather. "Well, hi, there, Mathias. I'm fine, thank you. How the hell are you?"

"I need to know, Sade."

"How did you know there was a dead vamp?" A heartbeat later, she guessed the answer. "He was one of yours."

"In a way."

"Who was he?"

"Simon Durden."

Sade detected no emotion in the master vampire's voice. "I didn't know him."

"No."

She bit her tongue and swallowed the snarl curling in her throat. Mathias was never loquacious in the best circumstances. When the subject turned to vampire politics, the man might as well be a mime on strike—no words, no gestures, no emotions. A long minute passed, the silence painful.

"Who did this?" Mathias bit out the words, sharp and deadly.

"Jeez, M. I've been on scene since just before the butt crack of dawn. We're not even sure of time of death—"

"The sun is up."

"He died last night, Mathias. Indoors." Something he'd said earlier finally registered. "Wait! What do you mean *in a way*? He wasn't your scion?"

"Not directly. But he was of my bloodline."

"Then you didn't feel his passing?"

"No."

"How did you know he had died?"

"Sade—"

"Don't *Sade* me, Mathias. How the hell did you know?"

"Language."

"Fuck that. How did you know?"

"His sire informed me."

"I need his sire's name and contact info."

"No."

"Dammit, Mathias."

"No. I will have the information you need at sundown. And no, you will not call. I will call you."

Dead air. He'd hung up on her. Seething, she marched into the warehouse.

"Simon Durden."

Toni glanced up, brow furrowed, her gaze insinuating that Sade had lost her mind. "What?"

"The vampire. His name is…was Simon Durden."

"Are you sure?" Roman leaned against the concrete wall, arms folded across his chest. His normally implacable face looked dubious.

"According to Mathias."

Caleb didn't quite gulp as he swallowed hard but it was a near thing. "Mathias? What's he got to do with this?"

"The decedent was of his bloodline."

Toni watched the three of them, her head whipping back and forth. "Do y'all know who Mr. Durden was?"

Sade crinkled her face as she stared at the ME, waiting for enlightenment. Before Toni could answer, Roman spoke up. "He was the Legate to New Orleans." He shared a meaningful look with Caleb.

"Legate? What's that?" Toni looked perplexed.

"That's the official magick representative in a neutral area," the gargoyle explained. "When a dispute arises between magicks, the Legate deals with it."

"We need to talk, Sade." Caleb appeared at her side and tugged on her arm.

"Okay."

"Not here."

Toni watched with interest, though Sade couldn't decide if it was due to the politics involved or to the preternatural men now standing on either side of her.

"Damn. How do I get to be you, Marquis?"

A snorted snicker escaped. "Trust me, Doc, it's not all it's cracked up to be." She allowed Caleb to lead her outside, away from nosy human ears. Roman followed close on their heels.

"What?" Roman and Caleb exchanged looks again. Sade fisted her hands on her hips. "What!" she demanded.

"Ariel." The name whispered from Roman's lips.

"What about him?"

Caleb growled softly. "He had...issues with the Legate."

Her eyes widened at the implication. "The dead *vampire* Legate. Laying inside that warehouse."

"Yes." The two men answered simultaneously.

"Three bodies, Sade. And Ariel had...issues with them all," Caleb added.

"Well...hell. Is there anyone Ari hasn't managed to piss off?"

CHAPTER SEVEN
HANDS OFF

CONVINCED SHE WAS NOW HOT on the trail of a magick serial killer—but not necessarily Ariel, Sade was prepared for anything, including the cold reception she was currently receiving from the NOLA Field Office Agent in Charge. Technically, she should have reported when she arrived on Sunday, but in the three days since and with bodies stacking up fast and furious, this was the first chance she'd had.

Sade faced down AIC Ed Burrows from across his cluttered desk. First problem, Burrows thought he was actually in charge. Second problem, he hated her guts. The feeling was mutual.

"Who died and made you boss?" Burrows glowered, the expression a pale comparison to what she was used to. Her godfather was a master vampire. His glower defined the word.

"The Old Man. This situation has magick nut dust all over it. That means it's mine."

Burrows muttered under his breath, questioning her parentage along with the FBI Director's.

"You're just jealous."

"Of you? Get real, Marquis. I don't play bend over the desk for anyone."

"Seriously? That's the best you've got?"

He muttered again. She refrained from reciting the rhyme about sticks and stones. "We have three dead magicks and the trail leads to your front door."

"Who cares? Freaking magicks."

"Oh. You mean besides the President? That freaking magick…elf?"

"Well, fuck."

Yeah, look who's bending over now. "No, thanks. I haven't had my shots."

New Orleans had always been a hotbed of the occult and the NOLA field office was Sade's first assignment out of the FBI academy. Burrows arrived not too long after. Luckily, she'd then gone to Los Angeles, serving under AIC George Bailey, who was now the current FBI Director. When the Big Rip occurred, the Old Man ended up in the head office after the former director—and a huge number of senior agents—took early retirement. Seemed they didn't want to change with the times. Soon after, she'd followed Bailey to Washington DC as a member of the newly-formed MAGIC Unit—Magical Activities, Grievances, and Inhuman Crimes, the joint project of the Justice Department and the White House after Congress enacted laws to protect the rights of humans and magicks both.

Dark days followed the rip and the losses on both sides were as ugly as any civil war. Under the new laws, MAGIC agents had jurisdiction anytime a crime involved a magick. Sade wasn't above putting Burrows in his place.

"Here's the deal, slick. I need an office, access to a computer, and no flack from you. I'll stay out of your way. You stay out of mine. Easy peasy."

Burrows turned an interesting shade of mottled red. If his tie hadn't already been loosened, Sade might have been tempted to help. As it was, she let him sputter. Better to get it out of his system now. He managed to stab his intercom and growl. Two minutes and two seconds later, a harried man appeared. He looked browbeaten and wary. She smiled at him and noted that he cringed. Damn. Her reputation obviously preceded her arrival. And she hadn't even killed someone. Lately.

"Tell Evans what you need. And get the hell out of my office."

"Your wish is my command. Not." She smiled at the nervous Evans. A real smile. He didn't relax. Huh. Maybe Caleb was right and she needed to work on her people skills.

"And keep that damned mutt of yours on a leash!"

Sade managed to walk out without either sucker punching Burrows or slamming the door. Maybe her people skills were okay after all. Out in the hallway, with the door to Burrow's office closed, she held out her hand for a shake. "Sade Marquis."

Evans stared at her hand and blanched. He reminded her of a mouse trapped by a rattlesnake. Yeah, her reputation was intact. Not that she'd been particularly worried.

"Regardless of what you've heard, Evans, I don't bite." She added "much" under her breath. "And Burrows shot himself. I wasn't even in the room when it happened."

That got a snicker from the man but he wouldn't meet her eyes. Evans led her through the labyrinth of cubicles, offices, and conference rooms. He finally stopped and pushed open a door. Inside a ten by ten office, Sade found a desk bare but for a computer and phone and a chair that had seen better days. Home sweet home. It would do.

"Thanks, Evans."

"No problem, Agent Marquis." Before she could comment on his formality, he scurried away.

After an hour of reading files, Sade gave up on a huge yawn and went in search of the break room and the coffeemaker. She felt like shit warmed over and wasn't sure even a hit of espresso would keep her eyes open. Sade missed the first feminine gasp but when every female support staff and half the female agents all peeked over their cubicle walls, she realized her reinforcements had arrived.

When they left the crime scene that morning, Caleb had accompanied what was left of the vampire's body to the morgue, much to the utter delight of the ME. Toni kept muttering something about giving Sade her first born as she watched the fit of Caleb's clothes. At some point, he and Roman had joined forces and were now strolling through the FBI offices. Sade figured no one who admired the allure of the two magicks would be working for the rest of the day. She waved to get their attention. Stepping into the break room, she filled a cup appropriated from the cabinet then led them to her temporary office.

"Steal some chairs," she murmured under her breath.

Caleb found an empty office, grabbed the two side chairs and hauled them into Sade's new space. Everyone settled and Sade flipped the monitor around where Caleb could read the report she'd been typing up. He read it as she fixed her gaze on Roman.

"Tell me."

Roman did her the courtesy of getting to the point of the interrupted conversation from that morning. "Ariel was here on Court business."

She blinked and made a dubious face. "This is New Orleans." Roman nodded. "Even *I* know there can be no politics here. What the hell sort of business?"

Roman arched a brow. "What sort do you think? We *are* discussing Ariel here."

Sade went shifty-eyed. "Oh. Hot monkey love business. And the Legate took offense?"

Before Roman could respond, her cell phone dinged. The ME's office. She held up a finger asking Roman to pause while she answered, "Marquis."

"Holy cannoli, Marquis. Do you realize who the victim is?"

"Hi to you, too, Doc. Roman, Caleb, and I were just discussing that."

"Oooh. Caleb is there?" Her voice sounded like melted butterscotch. Sade didn't appreciate the image that put in her head.

"Focus, Dr. Allison. Do you have time of death yet?"

"Oh, yeah. Uhm…no. Vampires don't exactly have liver temperatures we can measure. But that's not why I called. I never finished telling you this morning since the big guy interrupted me. I need to tell you about who Simon Durand was. Is. Well, who he used to be anyway." Toni rushed on without giving Sade a chance to respond. "He is…was *Judge* Simon Durand. The guy was legendary back in the day. And then he disappeared. Rumor was that he'd been attacked in his office at the courthouse. There was blood everywhere and everyone figured he was dead, his body just so much gator bait out in the bayous because it was never found. But evidently, he survived. Sort of."

"When did this happen?"

"Back in the thirties." The doc rifled through some papers. "I have his death certificate. The original one. June sixteenth, nineteen thirty-six. How the hell am I going to file a second death certificate? Of course, we didn't know about vampires back then. I'm just blown away by this all."

Sade leveled her stare on Roman. He didn't flinch. He didn't blink. Winning a staring contest with a gargoyle wasn't easy. "Call up to Health and Human Services in DC. There's a regulation to cover this, I'm pretty sure. Anything else?"

"I've sent samples to the lab but it'll be at least a few days before I have a clue about the type of acid or cause of death. Any ideas on figuring out TOD?"

"Yeah. I have a source. I should know something after sundown."

"I'll be here. Uhm…do me a favor? Tell Caleb hi for me."

She rolled her eyes. "Caleb? Your new girlfriend, the assistant ME for Jefferson Parish, says hi. I bet she's making googly eyes and sighing, too."

"Dang, Marquis. You go for the jugular, girl. I didn't know he was taken."

"Sade!" Caleb looked ready to throttle her.

"What time you getting off, Doc? Caleb will be there to take you. To dinner."

If Toni was blushing as much as her partner, Sade bet she'd need to set the thermostat of the air conditioner in the autopsy suite to chill out.

"Eight o'clock."

"You heard her, Caleb."

"I'll be there."

Yup, that was definitely a sigh coming through the speaker. Hanging up, Sade glared at the unmoving gargoyle. "You have some 'splainin' to do."

CHAPTER EIGHT
HERE BE DRAGONS

NIKOLAS CONSTANTINE, DRAKON of the Kholkikos Clan, stared through the plate glass window. On the other side, two dragonets splashed in the rooftop pool of the Hotel Monteleone under the watchful eyes of the royal nanny and a watch dragon. He straightened the cuffs of his Egyptian cotton dress shirt below the sleeves of his bespoke Italian suit. His fingers stroked the emeralds in his cuff links, an idle motion of which he was completely conscious. He pushed on the door and stepped out into the humid air. New Orleans was always humid, no matter the time of year but in the summer and late fall, it was downright steamy.

"Nikos! Come play wif us!" Eleni, the four-year-old princess of House Helios splashed water in his direction. He sidestepped the spray without effort.

"You can't call him Nikos. He's the Drakon." Prince Sotiris, two years older, thought he was infinitely wiser than his little sister.

"Ha. You have to call him Drakon. I get to call him Nikos. So there."

Shouts and splashes ensued. Eleni swam like an otter, sleek and playful, avoiding her brother's attacks with a skill born from being youngest. Their nanny rose from the chaise she'd been sunning on and bowed her head.

"Drakon. We are honored by your visit."

"Will the children be ready to accompany the royals tonight?"

"Yes, sir. I'm allowing them to play now so their natural…exuberance will be less noticeable during dinner and the show."

"And you have plans for your night off?" He watched her shoulders stiffen and the brief look of panic that splashed across her face like a reckless spray of water. He already knew her plans but expected her to confirm them. No one in the royal household went without scrutiny. As Drakon, he was in charge of security and was the Clan's chief enforcer.

"I-I have a d-date, Drakon."

"Indeed."

What many would consider a lovely shade of rose crept up her throat and infused her cheeks with color. "He…" She gulped. "He is fae, sir. A member of the king's court."

Poor girl. Ariel Daoine *was* a member of Oberon's court. The King's Seducer. While Aleta was pleasing enough in face and form, what would an experienced lover like Ariel wish with the girl? The fae was up to something, but for his life, Nikos could not figure out what.

"Where is he taking you?"

Dragons protected their females. Instinctually. Fiercely. Yet even he, as hide bound as he was in tradition, had to admit that chaining them in their rooms did nothing to help.

"To the Natchez. It is a riverboat. A paddlewheeler." Her eyes glowed with excitement. "For dinner and a cruise to see the lights." She held her body tight, curling in emotionally if not physically as if waiting for a blow.

"There will be dancing."

Her head jerked up and she stared at him, stunned by his remark but also looking hopeful. He offered a softening of the glitter in his eyes as encouragement. "You know what this fae is, Aleta?"

Her blush deepened. "Yes, Drakon. He is known as the King's Seducer but when the children grew bored of waiting in line for muffulettas, he bought them for us and brought them to us at the river so we could eat and watch the boats."

Odd that their guards did not do so. "Where were Stavros and Xan?" The girl refused to meet his gaze and her breathing and heart rate sped up. What guilt was she hiding? His tone left no room for anything but an answer as he said her name. "Aleta?"

"Xan…uhm…he was with Princess Nerine. She didn't want to stay with us. There was a store. Across the street. And then…" Her voice trailed off in fear.

He placed one finger under her chin, a gentle request to look at him. She raised her eyes first and then, somewhat heartened by his expression, she raised her head. "Nerine is headstrong, Aleta, and chafes at the constraints placed upon her. She is a royal princess and you are the nanny. I understand this."

What he didn't understand was why Stavros, one of his best lieutenants, had not reported the incident. "Go on, *mikró*. You are not in trouble. Tell me what happened."

Aleta swallowed hard, her throat working to get saliva around the constriction threatening to cut off her breathing. Fear wafted around her like the stench from a restaurant's dumpster. "There was a scene. In the store. Nerine wanted some article of clothing so she walked out with it. Alarms went off. Stavros…he had to go to fix it. *Ta micra*—the little ones. They were restless. You know Prince Sotiris. He stands still for nothing. Eleni was fretting and hungry. The line was long but both insisted they wanted only the muffulettas from this place. Ariel, the fae, he was in line before us, but he heard. He didn't seem offended by the children. Instead, he simply ordered sandwiches for all of us."

"All?"

"Yes, Drakon. All. Including Stavros, Xan, and Princess Nerine."

"So then you all went to have a picnic on the river."

"Well…not at first." She gulped again and her fingers twisted her lace swimsuit cover into knots. "He—Ariel pointed out the way. He stopped and spoke to Stavros. Then he joined us. Ariel. Not Stavros. Eventually, Xan arrived, too, but Stavros left. He escorted the princess back here to the hotel."

An incident involving the spoiled princess, witnessed by mundanes, and his men hadn't thought to mention it? This was something to be discussed with his security team, not the royal nanny.

"So then Ariel asked you on a date?"

"He said he understood the importance of my duties but if I should receive some time off, he would like to see me again, to show me some of the sights without the dragonets."

"So you contacted him?"

She dipped her head in a hesitant nod. "I did, when I discovered I would have this evening free. He suggested dinner and the cruise. I did not think, Drakon. I will notify him and cancel."

Nikos would have to be a right bloody bastard to ignore the yearning in her voice. She was a nanny. A servant of the royal court. There wasn't a dragon alive who would look at her as a woman. His gaze roamed over her, apprising her honestly. By human standards, she was lovely. Doe-eyed with ash blonde hair, she wasn't tall and her body was softly rounded in all the places a woman should be. Her skin glowed faintly pearlescent and her face was that of a gamin— young and innocent. She would be attractive to any man but a dragon.

"There is no need, Aleta. The free time is yours to do as you wish so long as you and the Clan remain safe." Her soft gasp and hesitant smile was reward enough. He seldom gave good news and he was surprised by the way his heart lightened at her delight. "Enjoy your evening."

"Thank you, Drakon. Thank you."

He turned on his heel, dodged another splash sent his way by the enterprising dragonets, and nodded to the watch dragon near the door. At least *he* understood his duties. Time now to deal with Stavros and Xan.

CHAPTER NINE
ONE OF THOSE DAYS

"HELLO, I WILL BE YOUR server tonight. My name is Eric." He handled the crystal water pitcher like a pro as he filled Sade's glass. "Our special tonight is the pecan-crusted sock-eye salmon braised in avocado butter, topped with lemon grass and bean sprouts."

"I'll have a filet mignon, rare, and horseradish, please. Real horseradish. And a baked potato with everything."

He sniffed, grabbed her menu with a flourish, and snapped it shut. Eric muttered, "Whatever." as he walked away.

"Yeah, whatever," she echoed. Just what she needed—a waiter with attitude. Granted, the place was a five-star restaurant but a man with softer hands and a better manicure—not that she ever got a manicure—always rubbed her wrong.

After he disappeared into the kitchen, she watched the other patrons. No one had a clue. Why should they? They were only human. Eric? Eric was a horse of a different color. A pooka to be precise, though she'd never met a preternatural of his particular flavor who should have been on "Queer Eye." Well, except maybe Harvey. He thought he was a rabbit and went around in a white fur coat when in human guise.

Eric came out of the kitchen balancing a tray on one hand and shoulder. He was actually pretty good at this waiter gig, considering he resembled a horse when his glamour slipped. Pookas were known for their mischief. The only magical beings more impish were imps. He headed Sade's way. His eyes narrowed and she could almost read his puckish thoughts. She eased back the placket of her jacket. Her badge flashed in the candlelight. He slid her salad plate in front of her. Gently.

"I guess you've caught me," he whispered. "I'm no leprechaun so don't be thinkin' I've a pot of gold or wishes to be grantin'." His accent was a dead giveaway before he cleared his throat and continued. "Besides, the statute of limitations has run."

"Hey, all I want is my steak."

"You aren't here for me?"

"Nope."

He returned ten minutes later, cleared her salad plate and left her steak in its place. "Enjoy your meal."

Sade cut into the beef with the intent of eating and getting gone. She hated dining alone but finding fast food in the French Quarter was an exercise in futility. Caleb was on a date with Dr. Toni. Roman was…wherever he went when he was dodging Sade's questions.

Her phone beeped with an incoming text message. From Mathias. Yeah, so much for calling. Why the hell were the men in her life avoiding talking to her? She opened the message and read.

Simon died at 03:27:46. Yes, his sire is certain. No, I will not share that information. You do not need to speak with him, nor will you. It is enough that we know the Legate is dead. The Council will take steps. Your investigation stops now.

"The hell you say, you fangy sonavabitch."

"I beg your pardon?"

Sade looked up from her phone. And up some more. The man standing at her table put a crick in her neck. His pale blue eyes flashed silver in the golden lights of the chandelier above her table. That same fixture cast a soft halo around him and she had to squint to get a better look. His close-cropped hair was of indiscriminate color and he wore his expensive suit like a second skin.

She really wished Caleb was with her. He'd sniff out the magick's flavor in a heartbeat. Or Roman. Roman was older than dirt. Hell, Roman *was* dirt. Or granite. Same thing.

Emeralds set in a buffed, silver metal—platinum if Sade had to guess—sparked at the magick's cuffs. A watch that probably cost six-months' worth of her salary gleamed on his right wrist. Impeccable. If she had to describe him in one word, that would be it. Impeccable. And sexy. Oh, mama, the man was that.

His full lips curled into a knowing smile and his eyes narrowed almost imperceptibly as he gazed at her. "I hope you were not speaking to me. I am neither fangy nor a son of a bitch."

Eric appeared with an ice bucket and stand, making a show of setting it beside the table and decanting the champagne. Sade watched with one brow arched before turning a lazy gaze toward the man still standing expectantly.

"What flavor are you?"

His eyes narrowed as he stared down at her and a layer of his sophistication slipped slightly. Nikos briefly wondered if he'd made a mistake. Then her emerald green eyes snapped and he knew she was most definitely something beyond normal experience, even for the Drakon of the Kholkikos Clan.

"Nikolas Constantine. May I join you?"

"Sade Marquis. No, you may not."

Her voice vibrated through him and the small mark at the corner of her mouth beckoned him with each word. Ignoring her denial, he pulled out a chair and sat.

"Seriously? What part of *no* do you not understand?"

"Your steak is getting cold, Sade."

"That's Special Agent Marquis to you." She put her palm on the table and when she moved her hand, her badge case flipped open to her ID. "FBI."

If he'd been standing he would have backpedaled a few steps. He'd been so enthralled by her looks the import of her name had blown over him like a cloud playing peek-a-boo with the sun. Even more intrigued now, he leaned forward, holding her gaze.

"What brings the infamous Special Agent Sade Marquis of the FBI to New Orleans?"

Her mouth thinned and her chin raised a fraction. "Official business. And you haven't answered my question."

"What question would that be?"

"What are you, Nikolas Constantine?"

"I am Drakon of the Kholkikos Clan. You may call me Nikos."

The realization in her eyes was delicious. She knew he was dragon and she now knew exactly who he was within his world. Having a human so well in tune with the Realms could be entertaining. He watched as thoughts ricocheted around her brain. Purposely insolent, he studied her. She would be tall when she stood. Slender, despite her broader shoulders, and with wiry muscles. Her hair reminded him of charcoal just lit, with small flames licking through its strands.

Her full mouth was made to be kissed, even as it hid its voluptuousness from the world. The mole at the corner drew his gaze and he longed to tease it with this tongue. Her chin held a very slight indenton before melting into a strong jawline leading to high cheekbones and to the one thing that drew him above all others. Her eyes. Eyes of emerald green, cut and faceted to catch the light. Rubies, diamonds, sapphires, amethyst and lesser gems all held a place in his treasure horde. But emeralds? Emeralds were his gem of choice.

His fingers curled into his palms, hands hidden in his lap. Her gaze broke for a moment and flickered across him. And he knew. The stories were true. Sade Marquis was unlike any other mundane. In fact, mundane was an insult. What had shaped her into the woman he now coveted? He would find out, sooner or later. Unlike many of his kind, he enjoyed pillow talk—the give and take of secrets and desires. He would especially enjoy it with this intriguing human.

"You should try the champagne, Agent Marquis. It is an excellent vintage."

"The answer's still no."

He wanted to touch her. To kiss her. Before she could react, he leaned across the table, captured her cheeks in his palms, and bent his head to savor her mouth.

The kiss was deep, reaching into her soul. Her eyes remained open, glittering gems watching him. His eyes stayed fixed on hers. He slanted his mouth to brush his lips across hers before sucking in her bottom lip only to release it after a tiny nip. His tongue teased the spot, soothing and inflaming at the same time.

Her breath hitched and he deepened the kiss again, pressing his advantage. He would have her before the sun rose in the morning. She shifted beneath him, pressing closer and he froze.

"I'm not quite sure what will kill a dragon, though I intend to find out. I *am* sure the rounds I have loaded in my Beretta will certainly make you think twice." Sade's words whispered into his mouth as the barrel of her pistol pressed against his erection.

Nikos didn't breathe. As much as Sade wanted to look away from his silvery gaze, she knew she'd lose her advantage if she did. The dude was a fucking dragon, even if he was in human form at the moment. His magic shimmered across her and she fought the urge to shiver. And to lean back into his kiss. Holy hell the man could kiss.

Contrary to popular belief, she wasn't an ice queen. She liked men. A lot. She appreciated their form and function. A lot. She had girly bits that turned into slutty cheerleaders shaking their pompoms at inopportune times. Like now. But she would not be manipulated. Especially not by some alpha-magick-hole with a God's-gift-to-women stamp on his forehead.

Nikos eased away but he kept his gaze tangled with hers. She'd won the first round though it damn sure didn't feel like a win to her. Sade remained almost as still as death, sipping small amounts of air so her hand would be steady if she had to pull the trigger. The dragon could strike and overpower her between this breath and the next but she'd dealt with magicks her whole life. While her reflexes were only human, her finger had not eased off the trigger. A deep breath and his dragonhood would likely be beyond healing.

His fingers slipped from her cheeks with one last, longing tap of an index finger against her chin. His eyes held both amusement and wariness, not a good combination for the person on the receiving end of that gaze.

"You win, Sade Marquis. For now." Nikos straightened, stood, and backed away.

The atmosphere in the room lightened and expanded. Glasses clinked, the low murmur of conversation swelled. Had time stopped? Or had the crowd realized something terrible was about to happen and they'd all stilled in anticipation? Sade couldn't tell as she watched the elegant man leave the room, the eyes of every woman watching his departure with longing.

Sade speared a bite of steak and chewed the flavorless chunk of beef. Her appetite had disappeared but she needed something in her stomach. Forcing another bite into her mouth, she chewed, swallowed, and repeated until her plate was empty.

Eric appeared with her bill. Flipping open the leather case to look at the tab, she expected an amount far too expensive for her per diem. Instead, she found an embossed business card. There was one word on the back, in a flowing, elegant script.

-Someday-

CHAPTER TEN
DECISIONS

KRISTIAN ST. JOHN FACED the semicircle of magicks, spine straight, chin jutting in defiance, eyes unblinkingly fixed on Mathias DeVries. Mathias let Sinjen's insolence slide for the moment. The man had not grown soft through the years, despite his proclivity for more cerebral pursuits. A lethal warrior still lurked beneath the modern exterior draped in a designer suit. St. John's eyes sparked like a blue flame, the only sign of his barely controlled fury.

"No."

"You refuse us?" Crevan's voice rumbled through the marbled chamber. As *Le Viele* of the gargoyle realm, Crevan presided over Council meetings.

"Yes."

The eyes of the council members focused on Mathias. He ignored them, his unwavering attention on the other vampire. "You deny *me*?" Mathias reined in his anger, which warred with a certain amount of pride in his progeny.

"Yes." Sinjen didn't blink.

"You understand the import of your words and actions?"

"Yes."

The other members stirred, their mutters and furtive glances becoming irritating. Mathias waved a negligent hand. "Any further discussion of this shall occur before the Vampire Conclave. I will deal with you there. Until you are summoned, stay out of my sight."

"As you wish." Sinjen pivoted, presenting his back to the Council as he strode from the room.

The arrogant prick had style. Mathias would give him that. After all these years, Kristian St. John remained an honorable man. Even so, his actions did not help the situation at hand. Coercing him to create another scion to become Legate should have been simple. Sinjen's attitude complicated matters.

Across the way, Queen Titania cleared her throat. Oberon couldn't be arsed to attend the meeting. "This still leaves us with the dilemma of appointing a new legate." Her voice lashed out as sharp as a barb-tipped whip. "I thought you had your minions under control, Mathias, and since one of mine was murdered, I want satisfaction."

Romulus Jones, the werewolf representative, growled. "We lost one of ours, too, Titania."

"You will address me with respect, you mangy—"

"Enough." Crevan did not raise his voice. He didn't have to. The word he uttered sliced through the tension like a bullet through water. "Tensions are running high. Need I remind you the chamber of the Concilium Magicae is also neutral ground?"

The peloton of gargoyle warriors standing behind him added emphasis to the question. While most had been used to transport those magicks unable to teleport, a phalanx of them remained armed and watchful—the Council Sentinels.

Theron Helios, the dragon Chancellor, stretched and flexed, his power barely contained by the human form of his glamour. He yawned, refusing to hide his boredom any longer and said, "I propose we call once again upon the gargoyles. Name one of the Sentinels as the Legate."

The murmurs rose to the volume of mutters. Mathias looked thoughtful as he assessed the other delegates. No one ever wanted to play poker with Rom Jones. His expression remained blank. Titania bit back a retort as did the elf sitting beside her. The wizard and witch huddled on the opposite end of the curved table, whispering to each other. Crevan held his own counsel as he watched.

"We propose it be so," the witch spoke up. She remained on her feet, facing down the scrutiny of her peers. "Ever have the gargoyles acted as messengers, as negotiators and guardians, as ambassadors. Does it not make sense that one act as Legate to New Orleans?"

"Do you have a name to submit, Mistress Moon?" Mathias had his own poker face in place now.

The witch glanced at the wizard before retaking her seat. He slowly rose to his feet and stared at the phalanx. His gaze flitted across each face, obviously searching for one in particular. When he didn't find the face he sought, a moment of indecision flickered in his expression. "I do not see the Sentinel I seek. Is he not present?"

Crevan arched a brow for a moment and then furrows formed on his forehead. "Roman Montagne?"

The wizard nodded, relief washing over him. "Yes. That one."

Titania sniffed, her lips thinning as she prepared to disparage both the wizard and Roman but the elf beat her to the draw.

"He has long served in all the realms, *Le Viele*." Llewellyn Gruffydd, the Elf *Arwain*, ignored Titania's glare.

"He has, *Arwain*." Crevan's voice gave no hint of his thoughts.

Theron, the dragon, nodded. "I vote aye."

His vote was endorsed swiftly by the wizard and the witch. Mathias nodded, acquiescing to the group. Titania glowered but said nothing, realizing she was outnumbered.

"I will notify the Sentinel." The gargoyle glanced around the chambers. "Is there other business to come before the Concilium?"

Titania cleared her throat again. "I do not want the human involved in the investigations." She looked regal and full of disdain as she turned her attention toward the vampire.

Mathias ignored her dig. His feud over Sade was with Oberon. In the intervening years, they'd come to an uneasy truce, much to the Queen's chagrin. Of course, she'd been the one to end the constant raids, which sent the human child into the nether realms as each side tried to keep her hidden. Mathias held no shred of guilt for what he and Oberon had done to Sade. Marking her had been expedient at the time and their actions now benefited all the realms.

"But she's so very good at her job, your Highness." He dipped his words in oil before coating them with sugar. "Though she may take offense when she learns you once sent your courtier to kill her."

Titania's expression did not change. "I should have ended her miserable existence when I had the chance. But you will remember I did not."

"Let her do what she does, Titania." Mathias shed any attempt at politeness. "No one is better suited to discover who is behind these deaths." He leaned back in the padded chair and steepled his fingers in front of him. "Unless you are afraid of where the finger might point?"

"Ha! I am afraid of nothing that brat can do. Fine. Let her continue. But we will not leave punishment to the human authorities." She rose and blinked out of existence before anyone could reply.

Gargoyles stepped forward to escort the witch and wizard, moving to the center of the chamber before teleporting. The dragon saluted the gargoyle and vampire before he teleported. Crevan dismissed the remaining Sentinels, leaving the two of them alone. Mathias gathered his thoughts while the gargoyles silently filed out.

"The world is spinning out of our control, Crevan."

"Perhaps."

"What have you discovered about these latest tremors disrupting the Veil?"

"Nothing. And that concerns me."

Mathias stared into the distance, his thoughts turned inward. "I am alarmed as well, Old One."

The weight of his introspection bowed his shoulders for a moment. He would need to deal with his scion's rebellion soon. And Sade's fate was never far away from his thoughts.

"We will do what we must, Mathias, when the time comes. As we have always done."

The vampire heaved out his chair and plodded off the dais to the gargoyle who appeared to transport him. "Would that Fate choose other champions, Crevan."

A moment later, he and his escort disappeared. Crevan stared at the empty spot, his brow furrowed. "Fate doesn't choose, Mathias. She would be far kinder."

CHAPTER ELEVEN
CAUTION

SLEEP CAME HARD UNDER the best of circumstances. In the middle of an investigation? Sade didn't know why she even tried. The hotel phone rang and she snagged the receiver from the bedside table.

"This is the front desk. Sorry to disturb you, Miss Marquis, but you have a visitor on the way up."

Sade groaned. If it was that freaking dragon, she was going to burn his ass. "Who?"

"He said his name is Roman—"

"It's okay. He's working with Agent Jones and me."

"Thank you. Again, sorry to disturb."

Moments after she hung up, Roman knocked sharply on the door. She opened it and stepped back.

"You look like hell."

"Well, gee, thanks, Roman. Good evening to you, too."

"What's happened?"

"You mean besides my run-in with a dragon at dinner?" She shrugged. "Or three murdered magicks? Oh. How the hell do I kill a dragon, anyway?"

"You take his heart."

"Easy peasy." She crawled up on the king-sized bed but Roman remained by the door, leaning against the wall. "Are you going to tell me about Simon Durden?"

"Are you going to tell me about the dragon?"

"Nothing to tell. He tried to pick me up at dinner. I declined the invitation." Sade wasn't sure why, but she refrained from mentioning the dragon's parting shot.

"As you know, Simon Durden was turned by one of Mathias' scions."

"I want to know which one. And why."

"Mathias has refused to reveal who to any but the Council. The why is simpler. The old Legate died and for awhile during the twenties, New Orleans was in turmoil. In the thirties, the Council negotiated a new compact. New Orleans was to remain neutral ground."

"So…why just one Legate? And what exactly is a legate again?"

"The Legate is the Council's representative. He or she presides over neutral territory, settling disputes and handing out punishments for infractions. Finding a legate is always a difficult task as the various races refuse to give any other the upper hand. In this case, a vampire who is a direct descendant of Mathias turned Durden. As a human judge, Durden's record was spotless. He was a fair man. He would make a fair legate. The only way to take away his mortality was to turn him."

"Why do I have the feeling no one was very happy about the solution proposed by Mathias?"

"Yes and no. Mathias has one direct scion who, while being a master, had never turned a human."

"Wait. What?" Sade stared at Roman as her mind shifted through the implications. "I thought vampires drew their power from those they turned." Roman nodded. "So how the hell did this guy become a master?"

"That is a question for Mathias to answer. The point is, the Council agreed that this master who had never turned a human would turn Judge Durden, and the judge would become the Legate of New Orleans. Forever."

The implications hit. "Well…crap."

"Crude observation but true."

"Damndamndamn. This means New Orleans is up for grabs again. Are we looking at war, Roman?"

He stared past her. She'd opened the curtains to the vista of the French Quarter. "I don't believe so. The Council is meeting to name a replacement." If gargoyles sighed, the huff of breath Roman released would qualify.

"There's something else, Roman. What is it?"

His gaze shifted slightly to meet hers. "It is about Ariel."

"Of course it is. It's always about Ariel. You started to say something this morning at the scene. Spill it, Roman."

"He was banned from New Orleans for a time."

"By the Legate?"

"Yes."

"Go on."

"Admittedly, he was stuck under that proverbial rock. He could obey his king or the neutrality law. Oberon sent him here to seduce a rival's mistress. Under the rival's nose. There was a...scene."

"This was before the Big Rip."

"Yes."

"Fuck. How long was he exiled?"

"Fifty years."

"When was the ban lifted?"

"Last week."

Her chest tightened at the implications.

"I'm sorry, child, but you must consider him a suspect."

"Just because he had ties to all three victims?"

"Not just ties, Sade. The Legate had banned him. He had a blood feud with Alvin."

"And Victoria Smith? From what I gathered from Caleb, she and Ariel mutually parted and remained friendly. Ari obviously cared about her. Why would he murder her? And in such a way? Filling her veins with silver and then cutting off her head?"

She pushed off the bed to pace. Concentrating, she chewed her lips. After several trips to the window and back, she stopped and stared at Roman. "I'll have to bring him in. Hold him until I can prove he's innocent."

"He may not be guilty of these crimes, Sade, but the fae has never been innocent."

Conceding that point by her silence, Sade grabbed her cell to call Caleb. It rolled over to his voice mail. "Leave a message."

"Yeah, I'll leave a message. Get your ass back to the hotel, Caleb. We have—" *Beep* Sade sputtered and stared in disbelief at the phone in her hand. "He cut me off." She turned wide eyes to Roman. "Oh. My. God. He's getting some. He and the ME are doing it. Right now. Going at it like—"

"Stop. I do not need that image in my head." Roman pushed off from the wall and reached for the doorknob. "Tomorrow is time enough, Sade. You need to sleep."

She barely refrained from rolling her eyes as she muttered, "Yeah, like that's gonna happen."

Roman softened his voice as he watched her, concern radiating from him. "I can help with that, Sade."

Shaking her head adamantly, she answered, "Not gonna happen. Magic doesn't work on me, Roman. You know that. And I don't do potions, draughts, or drugs."

He reached out, brushed an affectionate finger across her cheek, and tucked a stray lock of chestnut hair behind her ear. "You still need to sleep, Lady Sade. Promise me you will try? Put aside your worry for tonight. As far as the fae is concerned, what will be, will be."

She shrugged but followed Roman to the door to let him out. Sade locked up and flipped the security bar after he departed. Leaving the curtain open, she switched off the light and climbed into bed. The pillows bore the brunt of her aggression before she stabbed the on button of the remote control. Lights from the television screen flickered, creating more shadows than dispelling them.

After flipping through the available channels, Sade returned to a sports channel and left the TV on with the volume turned low. Convinced she wouldn't sleep, she read the trailer on the bottom of the screen until her eyelids drooped and she crept into a light sleep.

Nikos stared at her attire. A gray tank and shapeless cotton sleep pants could not hide her allure. Not to him, though he wondered why she would place so little value on the things making her such a beautiful woman. She'd gathered up her magnificent mane and secured it with a hair tie. His palms itched to loosen it, to tunnel his fingers through its silken mass. On her back, she lay sprawled across the bed, one knee bent slightly, the opposite arm crooked to cradle her head.

"Too many clothes," he murmured and she stirred. "Yes, *mikró mou*, my little one. You hear and respond to my voice."

He leaned over the bed and her skin pebbled as his breath washed over her. So sensitive. So alive. He traced her jawline with the tip of his finger. Her skin felt as exquisite as he'd imagined. Her neck arched as she followed his hand, craving his touch.

"Ah, *khriso mou*. You are truly my treasure." Nikos shed his clothes and settled on the bed next to her. "Come to me, Sade."

He gathered her into his arms, reveling in the way her body fit his. She was thinner than he normally liked, but her wiry muscles bespoke of strength. When he slipped inside her, she would welcome him into her depths. For now he was content to hold her, to kiss her temple and trace his hands along her body.

She nestled in at his side, her head on his shoulder. His cock thickened as her warm breath feathered through the hair on his chest. Many of his kind would only mate with other dragons, seeking their natural forms for the act of love. While there was something exhilarating about a mating flight, it could also be brutal, with rending claws and the male forcing the female to his will with teeth and claws, overpowering her with his size.

Nikos didn't want that. He wanted this human woman soft and pliable in his arms. His fingers explored the slim column of her throat then discovered the slope of her shoulder. Her rounded breasts nudged his chest with each gentle exhalation.

His treasure slept with her lips slightly parted. He longed to taste her again, to discover the silken heat of her mouth, and to feel the velvet of her tongue wrapped around his most intimate places. He cupped her breast and she stirred, her mouth opening wider. His lips brushed across hers, swallowing her breath. Curious, his hand slid down her side, mapping the hills and valleys of her body. He worried the knot on the string holding up her sleep pants until it loosened enough he could slip his hand in to tease through the soft curls covering her mound.

The scent of her sweet arousal perfumed the air and he broke their kiss to inhale it deeply into his lungs. She smelled of clove and rain, of gardenias and moss, sweet and earthy. His cock lengthened, hardened even more, as it sought her deepest secrets.

"Hey, you. Get offa my cloud."

Nikos reared back, his mouth thinning in anger. "Though there might be those who find your colloquialisms quaint, I am not one of them."

"Dude, this is my dream so get the fu—"

He covered her mouth with his, silencing her protests. Her hands planted against his chest and she shoved. To no avail. He was a dragon. A puny human could not dislodge him. Sade murmured into their kiss, squirming beneath him. His hands pushed up her top, fingers seeking more of her skin. He was lost in the moment and he closed his eyes as her passion enveloped his senses. Her knee nudged his thighs so he widened them enough she could slip her leg between them.

As soon as his legs widened, Sade grabbed his shoulders and rammed her knee into his balls. His teeth clicked together as a moan whooshed out of his lungs. She pushed and he rolled away enough she could get leverage to kick him out of bed. He landed hard. Sade didn't care.

"What the fucking hell?" She sat straight up in bed, panting. The TV still flickered but no naked dragon crouched on the floor beside her bed. Her heart pounded and she worked to get her breathing back under control. Sade didn't dream. Ever. At least not that she remembered. She grabbed the bottle of water on the nightstand and downed it. By the time she'd swallowed the last drop, her body had relaxed and her eyes felt heavy-lidded. She got under the covers this time then switched off the light.

"I suck at sex," she groused. "I can't even have a proper wet dream."

CHAPTER TWELVE
READ BETWEEN THE LINES

HOT SHOWER. CHECK. HOTTER COFFEE. Check. Cold shower. Yup. Colder water. Drank that, too. No matter what Sade did, she still felt unsettled. Shaky. Hung over. Thirsty. Needing something but not sure what. Wanting something but she didn't want to think about what that might be. She vaguely remembered a dream involving kissing and some heavy petting but the man's face remained blurred and her body felt...detached. Like it wasn't really hers. Which was ridiculous. If it wasn't her body, then whose was it? And who had appeared in her dreams?

Her phone played the opening notes of "Werewolves of London" and she opened the text from Caleb: *breakfast I'm starved*

Seriously? She typed out a reply: *You didn't get enough to eat last night?*

She received an emoticon in reply: ;-9. The sorry sonavabitch was smiling and licking his lips. Figuratively speaking. She would kill him. With her bare hands. The smug bastard. She slipped on her shoulder holster, clipped her badge to her belt, and grabbed a light jacket as she headed out the door.

"Breakfast. You want breakfast, Caleb?" she muttered on the way to the elevator. "I'm surprised the damn ME didn't give you breakfast in bed."

"She did."

Whirling, Sade nailed Caleb on the arm. "Don't fucking sneak up on me like that, you asshole."

Caleb exhaled and rolled his eyes. "Maybe the damn fae is right."

She stared at him, brows knitted in frustration. "About what?"

"Your language." He held up a hand to stay her next onslaught. "Who pissed in your cereal this morning?"

"Why should you care? You woke up with a smile on your face."

The elevator dinged and opened just as she spoke. Two women, gray-haired and spry, eyed Sade over the tops of their bifocals.

"There's certainly nothing wrong with that, young lady," one insisted, elbowing the other as they both smiled brightly at Caleb.

Ten minutes later, after Sade had leveled two hung-over tourists with her evil eye so they vacated *her* booth at Déjà Vu, she sipped on a café au lait and did her best to ignore Caleb. Jax slid plates onto the table, spun like a dancer to snag a full pitcher of ice water then filled their glasses. Sade managed to eat half of her breakfast before her phone rang.

Caleb stopped chewing on his steak to listen. He met Sade's look with a slight shake of his head and a lift of one shoulder. Then he concentrated on finishing his food as she wrapped up the conversation. She managed to chow down the rest of her French toast and chugged the coffee in her cup before she stood and tossed money on the table. She snatched the last piece of bacon on her plate and headed for the door, Caleb barely a step behind.

"Where we headed?"

"Hotel Monteleone."

"Dragons, huh?"

Sade stopped dead in her tracks. If Caleb was human, he would have plowed over her. As it was, he grabbed her upper arms to steady both of them as he stepped up beside her.

"Sade? What's wrong?"

71

Color drained from her face but she wasn't about to tell Caleb one blasted thing about her dream—which came rushing back in almost knee-buckling clarity as soon as he mentioned dragons. Why the hell had she been dreaming of that damned Nikolas Constantine? And a wet dream? Seriously?

"Nothing." She cleared her throat. "How did you know this concerned a dragon?"

"Because I know a delegation of them is staying at the Monteleone. Lucky guess." He started walking and she kept pace as he continued. "So did I hear right? One of them has gone missing?" Caleb studied her face. She wasn't telling him something but he couldn't figure out what. Normally, he could read her like a book.

"Uhm...yeah." Unfortunately, it wasn't the right one as far as she was concerned. "A nanny. From Audubon Park."

"The park? So why are we headed to the Monteleone?"

"Because that's where the fucking Drakon of the Kholkikos Clan and all the witnesses are."

"What about—"

"Local PD has the scene covered. There were kids there. With the nanny." Sade twisted her face into a perplexed expression. "What the hell do you call a baby dragon anyway?"

"Dragonet." Caleb's hand on her arm stopped her forward progress. "Sade, dragons aren't like other magicks."

"Really? I hadn't noticed."

"Can you hold the sarcasm for once? If you think the fae have a sense of entitlement, you've never dealt with a dragon. They're used to being the biggest and baddest and until circumstances forced them to play nicely with others, they pretty much did whatever the hell they wanted."

Sade arched a brow. "Wow, big bro. Strong language coming from you."

Caleb tried very hard not to sigh but it was freaking hard not to do around the infuriating woman he considered his sister of the heart if not of the flesh. "All I'm sayin' is tread carefully, okay? When they're in human form, all that magic is squished and twisted and compressed and when it explodes, it's never pretty."

Something in Caleb's expression caused Sade to swallow her smart retort. She offered a nod in subdued agreement. "Okay."

He read caution in her eyes and was satisfied. "Then let's go beard the dragon in his den."

"Wait. I thought lions got bearded. And what the hell does that mean anyway? Lions don't have beards. Neither do dragons." She widened the distance between them then glanced back. "Do they?"

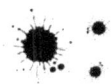

THIS WAS NOT THE WAY Nikos wanted to see the intriguing Fed again. In fact, he didn't want to see her at all under these circumstances. He wanted to hunt. Except he'd already quartered the park and there was no trace of Aleta. The prince and princess played in the next room under the watchful eye of Panos, the royal *magistros*. They seemed none the worse for the wear, in fact all but oblivious to the tensions mounting around them.

After disciplining Stavros and Xan for the incident with Princess Nerine, the two had stayed glued to the dragonets. Nerine had been shipped home for her infraction. That her picture appeared on the front page of the Times-Picayune newspaper convinced her parents to banish her back to the dragon realm for the time being. The teen had not gone happily. Not that Nikos cared. If he had his way, the royal family would stay safely ensconced on the other side of the Veil.

After escorting the dragonets back to the hotel, Stavros had returned to the park in hopes of picking up a trail. Next to Nikos, his lieutenant was the best tracker in the Dracos realm. Nikos chafed at the delay. Dealing with human authorities, even one as delectable as Special Agent Marquis, tried his patience in the best of times. He cursed under his breath. Before the Big Rip, his life had been so much easier. He simply fixed things. His way.

A watch dragon knocked on the door to the F.J. Monteleone Suite, the hotel's answer to presidential accommodations. The doors swung open and the woman who sent blood rushing south despite his best efforts strode in, followed by a man. Nikos schooled his expression to hide the snarl forming.

"Mr. Constantine." Sade nodded in his direction. "This is my partner, Special Agent Jones."

Every one of Caleb's senses went on alert as he eyed the tall man in the impeccable suit. How did Sade immediately know this dragon was the one in charge? And what did it have to do with her reaction earlier? He didn't miss the possessive gleam in the dragon's eyes as he perused Sade. His protective instincts ramped into hyperdrive. Despite the urge to go all alpha wolf, Caleb resisted. He also didn't offer his hand to shake. A smile snuck up on the corners of his mouth as the dragon's nostrils flared. Constantine had just gotten his scent.

"Agent...Jones." Nikos paused to give emphasis to his knowledge of who and what the werewolf was. The wolf just grinned at him, completely unimpressed.

"I love the smell of testosterone in the morning." Though Sade muttered it under her breath, both men heard her. And both bristled. She stared them down, daring either to speak. They wisely remained silent. "Why don't you tell me what happened, Mr. Constantine?"

Nikos shoved his hands into the pockets of his slacks to keep from reaching for the lovely agent. "If I knew what happened, you wouldn't be here."

Sade tucked her chin a fraction and stared at him as if she were a strict teacher peering over her spectacles at a recalcitrant student. Nikos did not appreciate being schooled. He inhaled slowly and clenched his hands, still safely hidden in his pockets. He wanted nothing more than to throttle her. Right after he kissed her. Or maybe before.

"Something occurred, Mr. Constantine, or I wouldn't be here. Your dragonets—"

"Not mine. The royal prince and princess."

"Okay." Sade arched a brow wondering why he'd been so quick to correct her on the parentage of the kids. Politics? Or... She immediately dismissed the thought it might be personal. "So...the prince and princess were in the park. What happened?"

"Their nanny disappeared."

"Disappeared? Like.. poof?" She raised her hands and made a gesture resembling an explosion with her fingers.

Nikos swallowed a growl. His eyes hooded as he stared at Sade. Was she baiting him purposely? "The prince and princess and their retinue were playing in the park. One moment, the nanny occupied a nearby bench, the next she was gone."

"No one saw anything?"

She didn't blink under his scrutiny. She was either very foolish or very brave. He stepped into her personal space, ignoring the werewolf bristling at her side. "You would not be here if they had. It is my duty to deal with such things."

Nikos moved closer still, watching Sade intently. Her scent wafted around him and he couldn't resist inhaling deeply. It was as he remembered—sweet and spicy and rich. One hand slipped from his pocket and reached for her of its own accord. She didn't back away, not even when he tapped the gentle indention in her chin with a fingertip.

"I am Drakon of the Kholkikos Clan. Do you understand what that means?" He pitched his voice low and purposely menacing.

"I am the agent in charge of the FBI's MAGIC unit. Do you understand what *that* means?" She arched a shapely brow and jutted her chin, almost daring him to touch her in more intimate ways.

Stubborn human. But he found himself both amused and frustrated. "As Drakon, it is my duty to deal with any attacks upon the clan."

"And it is my job to deal with you arrogant magicks when your crimes spill into the human realm."

Nikos laughed. The sound bubbled up from some hidden place in his gut. He wanted her now more than ever.

Her eyes narrowed and flashed like his favorite jewel as her infinitely desirable mouth tightened into a straight line. He wanted to kiss an exclamation point above her beauty mark.

"I'm so glad you find this situation humorous, Mr. Constantine."

He was not known as a patient man. Someone had taken something from him. He wanted to hunt down whoever had done so. Hunt and blood. Nikos allowed his glamour to slip just the slightest bit. The werewolf growled and feral red glowed in Jones' eyes.

Caleb stepped between Sade and the dragon. She had no idea what she was messing with. In a fair fight, he couldn't take Constantine. But he'd learned from the best. If it came down to it, the fight wouldn't be fair. And he had Sade as a secret weapon.

"I can deal with this, Caleb." At least she hoped she could. Her girly parts were certainly enjoying Constantine's alpha flare, the traitors. Intellectually, though, she was exasperated. She fixed the dragon with her most lethal stare. "And I will deal with this investigation, Mr. Constantine."

"No." He closed in on her, shouldering the werewolf out of the way.

Every instinct warned her to back away. This man was dangerous in far too many ways. He was a predator, like so many of the magicks. And he wanted her. That was obvious in his attitude, his expression, the way his gaze swept over her like she was a trinket to be bought. Yeah, like that was going to happen. Time to push back.

CHAPTER THIRTEEN
TALK IS CHEAP

"LEAVE IT ALONE." Sade didn't back down.

"Don't you mean leave *you* alone?"

She stared at the elegant man, taking a moment to really look at him. His pale blue eyes shimmered like sunlight on a clear mountain lake. His close-cropped hair matched the faint traces of shadow beard gracing his ruggedly refined features. Long, nimble fingers sparkled with jewels and the expensive watch on his wrist cost more than she made in a year. Hell, he wore another suit probably equal to several months' salary.

"Look, Mr. Constantine, I don't care who or what you are, this is my investigation. Your nanny—"

"The royal nanny, Agent Marquis. And need I remind you she was taken in front of the prince and princess?"

He radiated angry heat but Sade once again resisted the urge to step away, to seek cooler air to breathe. "What did they see?"

"Nothing."

Sade glowered at him. "Nothing? You're all bent out of shape because she was snatched right in front of them but they saw nothing. Hmmm. What's wrong with this picture? Need I remind you that withholding information in a federal investigation is a felony, Mr. Constantine?"

"Nikos."

"Excuse me?"

"I would prefer you call me Nikos."

"Forget it, slick. I'm here on official business."

"But you do go off duty upon occasion, Sade."

"That's Agent Marquis to you."

"We will have dinner together, *Sade*."

"Not happening."

Caleb watched in fascination, his presence obviously forgotten. He would step in if Sade got in over her head, especially since he didn't like the way Constantine was staring but at the moment, he simply kept score.

"It's my investigation, Mr. Constantine. Don't forget it." Sade pivoted, retreating toward the door. She preferred to think of it as a tactical withdrawal since it wasn't smart to piss off a powerful magick. If she stayed, she would. Guaran-damn-teed. Unable to resist one last question, she stopped at the door and faced him.

"You said the kids saw nothing but the nanny was snatched right in front of them. What did you mean by that?"

Nikos just managed to shutter the look of greed he'd allowed to overrun his expression. "Just what I said. One moment they were playing tag in the park. She was watching from a bench. The princess waved to her and turned to chase her brother. When she looked back, Aleta was gone."

"Gone. Gone like got up and walked away gone? Did anyone see her leave? Because if she didn't walk away, she must have poofed."

The way Sade's mind worked amused Nikos. Her reputation preceded her in the magick realms but meeting her was a revelation. His groin tightened. While he usually dallied with humans, few stirred his senses like this one.

He resisted the urge to smirk at her nonmagical term. "Yes, like poof, so it seems. However, contrary to popular belief, *Agent* Marquis, dragons cannot disappear into thin air. We can teleport into and out of our own realm but do not have the ability to do so from place to place within this one or into other realms. One of the guards checked that possibility immediately."

"Did they see anyone watching them? Or talking to Miss—" She pulled out a notebook but her brow furrowed.

"Aleta belongs to Clan Kholkikos as a servant of the House of Helios. As such, she has no surname."

"But you have a last name."

"Indeed. But, I am a different wyrm altogether. I am Drakon of the clan."

"So that makes you royal or something?"

"Or something." Amusement conquered anger. The corner of his mouth curled into a lazy smirk. What being Drakon made him was the enforcer for the clan. He guarded the royal family. He meted out justice to those in need. And he enforced the laws on those who broke them. He was Drakon—law keeper, law giver, and as such, above the law. Even human law, as this lovely upstart would learn soon enough. He would enjoy teaching her.

Sade read something in his expression she didn't like. Arrogance was a given but a darker emotion lurked there. Darker and…sexier. Despite a strong sense of self preservation—and with Caleb's advice that it wasn't smart to tease a dragon ringing in her ears—she marched back to Nikos and jammed her finger into his chest—his very muscular and hot chest. The tip of her index finger sizzled but she didn't move it.

"Last time, Mr. Constantine. This is my investigation. You are in the USA and in *this* realm, human law prevails. I will throw your scaly ass in jail if you interfere. Are we clear?"

"Have you not heard the sage advice from the very wise Anonymous?" Sade's brow crinkled, adding a cute exclamation point to her suspicious expression. "Meddle not in the affairs of dragons, for you art crunchy and good with ketchup." His smile turned sensuous as he added, "Though I much prefer a bottle of wine with an excellent vintage and caviar."

Resisting the urge to hit the egotistical magick, despite the balled fists at her sides, Sade offered a raised brow and her own smirk. The dragon's eyes fixed on her mouth. Good. The better to read her lips. "Ass. Yours. Jail. Last warning. If you think of something that might help my investigation, call my office. You have the number."

Sade executed a military-precise about face and strode toward the door. Nikos's heat followed her, licking out like a living thing. Goosebumps raised on her arms despite the warmth surrounding her.

"I want to talk to the dragonets. You will arrange that." She could almost smell her hair singe but didn't turn around.

"They are children, Agent Marquis." The chill in his voice would make a yeti proud.

Fire and ice. Sade didn't know whether to sweat or shiver. "They are witnesses. And all the guards who were there." She did turn to face him at that point.

"Prince Sotiris is six, Agent Marquis. And Princess Elani is four. I doubt they will be much help."

"The age of a magick is relative, Mr. Constantine."

Nikos resisted the urge to sigh. "If you will not call me by my name, Agent Marquis, then I will insist you call me by my title, as you have decreed I respect *your* rank. Dragon children are children. Talking to them would be the same as talking to human children of the same age. They were playing a game. They looked over and couldn't find their nanny. They alerted the guards. The guards searched but did not find her or any evidence of her departure."

Sade lifted her chin, her attitude going all I-told-you-so. "I expect those guards to appear at the FBI office this afternoon for interviews. Understood?"

"Perfectly."

How could the woman so infuriate him yet intrigue him at the same time? She should be frightened of him but she managed to hide her fear well. She stared into his eyes, didn't run from his fire, and didn't have the sense to get away while she could.

Once more, she approached the door to the suite. "I'll have more questions for you, too, *Drakon* Constantine. Don't leave town."

"Of course, Agent Marquis. I wouldn't think of it." Nikos watched her, every synapse in his body firing. Leaving town was the last thing on his mind. First, he would either retrieve Aleta, or if she was indeed dead, he would avenge her. Then he would assuage his desire for this maddening human.

The FBI agent never broke stride as the exit doors opened before her. Head high, Sade stepped out, followed closely by her pet werewolf, and the doors closed behind them. Damnation. Sometimes, his servants were too good at their duties. Once again, he contemplated the woman. Certain rumors were now confirmed. His magic had flared around her but she remained unaffected.

Interesting. A mundane immune to magic—though there was nothing mundane about this human woman. Her ability surely had the magicks in an uproar, though how convenient to have a human insusceptible to spells and glamours. She was a jewel he would own—sooner or later. He was a dragon. Dragons always hoarded treasure.

CHAPTER FOURTEEN
NO SECRETS WORTH KEEPING

THE DOORMAN LOOKED SHARP in his green jacket. He held the door and tipped an invisible hat with a white-gloved hand as Sade and Caleb exited the hotel.

"We need to get to Audubon Park."

"May I get you a cab?"

Sade glanced from the doorman to Caleb, who shrugged. He could jog to the park faster than most cars could drive, given the traffic. Sade hated walking anywhere. She nodded. "Yeah. That works. It'll be faster than trying to hitch a ride with NOPD."

The ride was almost tame. Traffic seemed light and the cab jousted with the St. Charles street car only a couple of times before turning onto Magazine Street and arriving at the entrance to Audubon Park. A marked NOPD squad car blocked their way. After much flashing of badges and a call to the cops' supervisor, they made it to the crime scene.

The dragon guard was hard to miss. His square jaw, steely eyes, and mane of thick brown hair belonged on a male model. His coiled strength shimmered just below the surface of his skin and the disdain he felt for the human police combing the park was tangible. His eyes tracked Sade from the moment she stepped out of the cab.

Once the formal pissing contest was over with the NOPD officers, she approached cautiously. "You one of Nikolas Constantine's guards?"

He nodded but didn't elaborate.

"Special Agent Sade Marquis and my partner Special Agent Caleb Jones."

His upper lip curled in a decent Elvis impression but he still didn't speak.

"Are you the one who poofed into the dragon realm to check to see if the nanny had gone home?"

"Dragons do not…poof."

Sade managed to keep a straight face as his lip curled even more. "There was no sign of her there?"

"None." He growled a little under his breath. "I have been ordered to cooperate. Do not insult my abilities to do my job."

"Okay. Don't insult mine. What can you tell me about Aleta?"

The dragon's brow furrowed and his eyes narrowed as they flicked from point to point around the scene, looking anywhere but at Sade. "What do you mean?"

"Is the question that har—" Caleb stepped on her foot, cutting off her snide remark. "Oww." She glared at the werewolf. "What do you know about her? Friends? Habits? Places she likes to go?"

"She is the royal nanny."

"And…?"

"And what?"

"That's all you know about her? Jeez. Is there anyone on staff she hangs out with?"

"No."

"Does she date?"

"She's the—"

"Yeah, yeah. The royal nanny. Does that mean she doesn't have a private life?"

Stavros' nostrils flared. "She was absent last night."

"Absent? Like AWOL or something? Did she miss a class and the teacher marked her absent? What the fuck does that—"

He held up a finger, snagged a cell phone from his pocket, and moved away while he made a call. While his attention was diverted, Sade leaned close to Caleb.

"Sniff around. See if you can pick up a trail, 'kay?"

Caleb nodded and casually approached two local cops standing nearby, ignoring the dragon as he passed. Sade watched the dragon talk on the phone. His expression remained shuttered but his body language spoke volumes. She suspected he was talking to Nikos Constantine. Her girly bits perked up and wanted to swoon. She ignored them. Nikos Constantine was an Alpha Jerk. She added a mental trademark symbol to the term and decided she had far too many man in her life who qualified for that title.

Stavros ended his call and returned to stand at attention in front of her. "The Drakon informs me I must answer all your questions and assist you in any way I can."

His words must have tasted like vinegar if his expression was any indication but Sade would take whatever cooperation she could get. "Good. So where was the victim last night?"

"Aleta. Her name is Aleta and she is the royal nanny." The air around Stavros shimmered with his magic and heat licked over Sade.

"Sounds like you have a personal interest in the girl. Were you the one she was absent with last night?"

Sade managed to duck and dance away as Stavros lunged at her. Her weapon appeared in her hand and she leveled it on the dragon's chest. "I may not be able to rip out your heart but I can damn sure blow it to bits, asshole."

Wisely, Stavros raised his hands and backed away. He was still angry but worked to contain the roiling anger mixed with magic. "My apologies, Agent Marquis." He bit out the words. "Your supposition is incorrect. I have no relationship with Aleta beyond the fact I am one of the guards assigned to the prince and princess while they are in this realm. The Drakon informed me that Aleta was off duty last night as the dragonets were with their parents. She had a...date."

"A date. A date with who?"

"According to the Drakon, she had a dinner date with a fae."

"A fae? Which—"

Caleb loped up, cutting off her question as he grabbed her arm and tugged her away.

"Caleb, what the fuck?"

"You need to find Ariel." He kept his back to the dragon and his voice a mere whisper.

"Why?" She didn't keep her voice down.

He pulled her further away, casting a worried glance over his shoulder to check on Stavros. "You need to find him before the dragons do."

"Dammit, Caleb. Why?"

"Because his magic is all over this."

"Fuck."

"Yeah. This is bad, Sade. First Victoria, then that fae courtier and the Legate. Ariel had reason to go after all of them."

"But why would he decide to do this now, Caleb? And why Victoria Smith? They parted on good terms."

He rubbed his palm over his forehead, pushing back his shaggy hair. "I don't know, Sade. Maybe he wanted to hook up with Tori again and she turned him down."

A cawing laugh escaped despite her best efforts to compress her lips. "Seriously, Caleb? This is *Ari* we're talking about. The dude can walk down the street and have a whole gaggle of girls following him like love-starved zombies. I just can't buy into the idea that he'd hurt someone. Not unless he was threatened first."

Both of them kept track of the local cops, bystanders, and most important, the dragon. They pretended to compare notes as they discussed the situation.

"Stavros called Constantine to get permission to talk to us. Evidently, the vic had a date last night. With a…" Sade blinked and she snapped her mouth shut.

"Had a date with a what?"

Her lips alternately pursed then thinned as she stared over Caleb's shoulder. She answered reluctantly. "A fae." Caleb's eyebrows played hide and seek with his bangs. After a moment's hesitation, Sade stepped around him. "Stavros! Who did Aleta go out with last night?"

Prepared for his answer, she still winced when he replied.

"Ariel Daoine. The King's Seducer."

Sade inhaled through her mouth, sucking air deep into her lungs, and then breathed out through her nose. "Crap. I was afraid he was going to say that," she murmured for Caleb's ears only.

Caleb turned to watch the dragon. Stavros appeared to grow then shrink and his whole attitude pointed to a vain creature preening and showing off his attributes as he gazed around the park. Every female within viewing distance definitely perked up and noticed. Hair on the back of Caleb's neck ruffled as magic shimmered around the dragon. Trying to contain all that power in a human sized vessel was like dropping a Mentos into a liter of Diet Coke.

"This is bad, Sade."

"You said that already."

"It seems worth repeating."

CHAPTER FIFTEEN
DRAGGING DOWN

ARIEL HAD DISAPPEARED FROM the face of the earth—or at least the human realm part of it. Part of Sade rejoiced. As infuriating as he might be, truth be told she was fond of the asshole. But twenty-four hours had passed without contact. She pretended not to worry.

Caleb stood in front of her investigation board, hands shoved in his front pockets, posture somehow both slouched and on alert. He accepted the coffee mug she offered.

"If the dragon is a victim, why haven't we found her body?"

Sade stared at the victims' photographs and the notes she'd scribbled on the wipe-off board beneath each one. "Good question. Maybe she just ran away and Ariel was a ruse."

"A ruse. And that would be why he's MIA?"

"I really can't see Ari running off with a dragon."

"Especially not one owned by the royal house."

"Now see? That just pisses the hell out of me. How can they own her? And who decreed she was nothing more and could be nothing more than a servant and a...plaything."

"Her caste determined that, Sade."

"So this is like India now? With unclean castes and crap like that? That's bullshit, Caleb."

He winced at her anger. Part of him agreed but the magick in his DNA understood the way things worked. None of the magical realms were a democracy. And there was always a pecking order.

"Maybe in your world, Sade, but in theirs—"

"My world? What the fuck does that mean? It's the same world you grew up in, Caleb!"

He cut his eyes to her before turning his head to fully regard her. "No, Sade. It's not. You never did get it when we were kids. Or when I had to follow you to college or the FBI Academy."

Sade, suspicion and hurt warring in her expression, watched him without comment. She broke the staring contest first, jerking her gaze to the murder board and rubbing at a smeared spot of ink with her index finger. She flinched when Caleb laid his palm on her shoulder.

"You know I'm right, Sade. Deep down you know. Magicks *aren't* human. We don't think like you. Act like you. We don't behave like you." A dry chuckle rumbled in his chest. "Which is lucky for you personally. Means you'll always have a job."

He dropped his hand and gave her a gentle shoulder bump. Sade's stoic expression didn't change. Caleb bumped her again.

"Don't."

He nudged her once more. And then a fourth time. She finally nudged back, only harder, without looking at him. She always had to win. And he always let her. His alpha status should probably suffer because he gave in to her but what his pack didn't know wouldn't hurt him. Hopefully. Not that he cared. Much. He'd been away from the pack so long, he'd formed his own—with Sade, and to a lesser extent, Roman, and even Ariel. That thought made him want to laugh, but he managed to keep the mirth hidden. Ariel made a perfect pack omega.

"What?"

"What?"

Sade huffed out a breath and rolled her eyes. "You are thinking evil thoughts. I can fucking feel them radiating from your brain."

"Me?" Caleb did his best to look innocent before sobering. "He'll get in touch, Sade."

"I just hope it's not too—" Her phone chimed the theme from "Cops." "Marquis." She listened for a moment and then grabbed a marker from the white board and scribbled down an address. "Thanks, Detective. If any dragons show up, shoot them in the heart if they try to get into the scene." A moment later she added, "No, not kidding. Well, not entirely. We'll be there ASAP."

"NOPD found the nanny." Caleb made it a statement. He grabbed his jacket and held the door for Sade to precede him. They hit the stairs rather than wait for the elevator. It was only three flights down. As they exited, Caleb pulled keys from his pocket and hit the unlock button on the fob. A sedan near the end of the fleet row beeped.

Caleb opened the driver's side door. "Where we headed?"

"Downtown. Well, technically, the riverfront. There's a warehouse near the Crescent City Bridge."

"Roger that."

Sade hated not driving but she had to admit Caleb's werewolf reflexes were better suited for whizzing through traffic. Still, she was white-knuckled by the time they stopped in front of the large, two-story concrete building. A couple of police officers kept nosy tourists behind crime scene tape. The detective they'd met at St. Louis Number One waited at the front door.

"Who found her?"

The detective pointed to a group of school children huddled with their chaperons. "Field trip. Nobody knew she was real."

Sade blinked at that and then the implications sank in. "Oh hell no." She whirled toward Caleb and keeping her voice low, asked tersely, "Do dragons revert when they die?"

The look on her partner's face was enough to kick her pace into a trot.

The NOPD cop gamely kept up with them, though his breath wheezed in and out like a steam engine on steroids. Large roll-up doors opened onto a riot of color. And creatures. The place was filled to the rafters with the trappings of Mardi Gras—floats, costumes, props. Sade understood how a dragon might go undiscovered for twenty-four hours.

Slowing to a walk, she let the detective take the lead. More crime scene tape was barely discernible against the chaotic backdrop. A scaled dragon, in colors of fading blues and greens, almost seemed normal. Yeah, but for the gaping chest wound. Okay...so maybe it wasn't so easy to hide the body, Sade thought.

Dr. Allison flashed Caleb a coy smile as she delivered her report. "Cause of death is evident. Its heart—"

"Her." Sade interrupted.

"Her?"

"Her. I'll need to get someone from the dragon delegation to positively identify her but since only one dragon has gone missing in New Orleans, I'd bet my odds are pretty good when I say her name is Aleta and she disappeared yesterday from Audubon Park."

The assistant ME swallowed and edged a little closer to Caleb. "If this is a female, I don't think I want to see a male dragon in his real—"

A roar from the front of building cut Toni off before she could finish the sentence. Caleb shoved her behind him and she didn't argue. She gulped and resisted the urge to cling to his jacket. She didn't feel relieved when she glanced over at Sade. The FBI agent just looked pissed. That couldn't be good.

Sade was halfway to the door when one extremely angry dragon stormed into the room. Nikos Constantine looked ready to explode. Her hair lifted and crackled like she was standing in the middle of a whirlwind of static electricity. She spread her legs and squared her shoulders against the onslaught.

His eyes flared and Sade could almost see the flames licking deep inside them. She really needed to check with Caleb or Roman to find out if a dragon's heart was located in the same place as a human's. Her fingers tightened instinctively on the grips of her holstered Beretta. The magazine carried a mixed load—iron, silver, and high explosive. Surely one of the three would shred a dragon's heart if it came to that.

The air shimmered around him and heat licked at her as he halted in front of her. "Where is she?"

"This is a crime scene, Mr. Con—"

"WHERE IS SHE?" His roar rattled the paper maché decorations and the glass in the windows set high on the walls.

"What part of *crime scene* do you not understand, Drakon?" The collective gasp behind her didn't bolster her nerves but Sade wasn't about to back down. She stepped closer and almost faltered when Nikos backed away.

"I will not have humans gawking over her remains, Agent Marquis."

"We aren't gawking, Nikos."

That Sade called him by his familiar name registered somewhere in the depths of his rage. Nikos inhaled raggedly and fought for composure. That any dragon might see him lose it was a shame he would not consider. He was always in control. Always in charge. Except he wasn't. Not around this human woman and not of this situation. He had failed his clan and his guilt squeezed his heart with each beat.

Sade rolled her shoulders to ease the tension, recognizing that the threat had diminshed. She took another, more cautious step toward Nikos. "I'm sorry for your loss, Drakon. I understand you feel responsible for her but I promise she will suffer no disrespect at our hands. Once the investigation here is finished, I will release her body to you. Okay?"

Nikos rubbed his palm over his close-cropped hair. He didn't know if he should feel chagrined—a completely new emotion—or if he should allow his anger to rebuild. Then sadness settled around him and his magic flickered down to normal levels.

"This is my job, Nikos. And I'm really good at it. I will find who did this to her. And to the other magicks who have died."

"You have talked to the fae? To the King's Seducer?"

Sade mulled over her answer, taking long enough that the dragon's expression morphed into distrust. She decided a portion of the truth was in order. "Ariel is missing."

"And you do not find this suspicious?" His silvery blue eyes bored into hers.

"I find it concerning, Drakon." She lowered her voice. "I'm breaking protocol, Nikos, but Aleta is not the first. Another fae, a werewolf, and a vampire have all been murdered."

"You think a magick has done this?" His magic swelled again as his anger surged. Nikos watched Sade's sudden intake of breath with an interest that had little to do with the situation and everything to do with the shape of the breasts hidden by her tailored shirt.

"It could be a human perp, Drakon. I don't make assumptions. I follow the evidence. Wherever it leads. That's my job." She leveled a warning glare on him. "And I'm very good at my job." She turned and nodded to Caleb, who stepped forward to intercept the dragon.

Sade snagged the ME's arm and tugged her behind a float. "I can't let you do an autopsy."

Toni blinked at her. "I...uhm...that's a dragon. I think technically, it would be a necropsy and I'm not qualified." She inhaled quickly and continued. "Who the hell *is* qualified to dissect a dragon?"

"Shhhhh." Sade's eyes widened as she looked around to make sure Nikos couldn't hear their whispered conversation. "Don't even think that much less say it out loud. There are enough dragons in town to incinerate the Quarter." She dragged Toni further away. "Look, I just need to know whether it was some*thing* or some*one* that caused the wound and whether the heart was cut or ripped out. Can you do that?"

Toni nodded even though her heart danced the flamenco in her chest. "Yeah. I can do that. The skin looks like it was cut. Something really sharp because the hide and the muscle were sliced clean. No ragged edges. As for the heart, though, it looks like it might have been ripped out. I'll have to go back and look closer. I was just doing my preliminary when y'all got here." She inhaled several times and rubbed her palms up and down her thighs to dry them.

Sade offered a lopsided smile. "I wish I could say it gets easier dealing with them. It doesn't."

"Great."

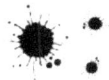

AN HOUR LATER, SADE sought out Nikos. "We've finished, Drakon. She's yours now."

His eyes narrowed and his lip curled in a snarl. "She has always been mine, Agent Marquis. You would be wise to remember that."

Sade bristled at the insinuation and the implied threat. "Need I remind you this is my investigation, Drakon? We've had this conversation. Stay the hell out of it."

Before she could react, his fingers curled around the back of her neck. Sade froze, not even breathing. Nikos leaned into her and inhaled, his nostrils flaring. "You smell of cloves and magnolias. I wonder if you taste as sweet?"

Her eyes dilated but he detected no fear. Anger. Arousal. Yes. But no alarm.

"Even dragons who play with fire can be burned, Nikos. *You'd* be wise to remember that."

"Will you scorch me, khriso mou?" He dipped his head and kissed her, holding her in place by the sheer resolve in his gaze. Her lips hardened beneath his, stretching into a tight, irritated line. He chuckled as he backed away, releasing her as he did so. The woman confounded him even as she banked the fires of his anger.

Pivoting on his heel, he walked off, leaving her to fume. When Caleb appeared at her side, she muttered, "Remind me to get a Greek-English dictionary." Nikos' laughter echoed down the hallway.

"Fucking magick hearing."

Out of Sade's human earshot, Nikos speed-dialed his phone. "It is her, Stavros. Make arrangements." He turned to watch the humans gathered around Aleta's body. "And bring me that damned fae."

CHAPTER SIXTEEN
WHO'S IN CHARGE

SADE PACED THE LENGTH of the paneled office, pivoted, and stomped back the way she'd come. Over and over.

"Desist, Sade, before you wear a hole in the rug."

She whirled to face the gargoyle standing in the doorway. Roman looked comfortable in these surroundings—fine woods, antiques designed to fill rooms with soaring ceilings, silk carpets, and an unparalleled view of the French Quarter from the window behind the mahogany desk. He was the last person she expected to see in the offices of the Council Legate of New Orleans.

"What are you doing here, Roman?" The answer dawned on her even as the words left her mouth. "Holy shit. *You're* the new legate? Why the fuck didn't you tell me?"

Roman peered down from his imperious height and his displeasure was plain to read in his facial expression. "I have been a bit preoccupied the past forty-eight hours and you have been embroiled in an investigation."

"Yeah, about that. I need you to find Ariel." His expression turned stoic but Sade had been playing poker with the gargoyle since she was old enough to shuffle. "You're like the new sheriff in town right? It's up to you to uphold the Council's edicts?" Roman's expression didn't change. "That's what I thought. I need Ariel in custody before the dragons find him."

Something flickered in Roman's flinty eyes and his face softened almost imperceptibly. "Do you truly believe Oberon would risk war with the dragons over his Seducer?"

"Argh!" Sade threw up her hands. "Of course not. Oberon couldn't be arsed. But do you really want the New Orleans' Accords broken?" She paced the room again. "The dragons can't go to the fae realm to get him. And if he has any fucking sense, that's where he's hiding but this *is* Ariel we're talking about. He doesn't have the sense God gave a turnip. If I know him, he's sitting here under our fucking noses laughing out both sides of his ass and thumbing his nose."

She paused for a moment, staring out the window. "This is important, Roman. Since the Veil ripped, humans have been playing catch up and doing a piss poor job of it. Face it. You magicks have us pretty much at your mercy. I don't want the Dark Days to come back when humans pretty much killed every magick they found out of fear and a misguided sense of self-preservation. Nor do I want to see your kind slaughter us."

"My *kind* has been protecting humans for a millenium, Sade." Roman's angry voice sounded like two blocks of just quarried granite crashing against each other.

Sade breathed, eyes closed, head back as she tried to loosen the crick in her neck. She blew out her breath, turned to face him, and opened her eyes. "Help me, Roman."

His heart contracted and didn't beat for a moment. Her eyes looked like liquid glass, her expression stark and worried. He remembered the angelic-faced toddler with wild chestnut hair and eyes the color of shamrocks on a summer's day. He'd watched wariness turn her eyes to brittle shards of glass glinting under a relentless noon-day sun. Of all humans, this one had more right to hate his kind than any other. Instead, she worked ceaselessly to protect magicks against the prejudices of fear and to bring justice into a lawless world.

"As you wish, Lady Sade." She swayed slightly, as if that once innocent child in her psyche craved the safety of his arms but then the woman asserted herself—the woman who could stare down an enraged faerie queen or a blood-thirsty vampire and walk away unscathed. Her scars remained deeply disguised. He reached for her but settled for tapping his index finger against her chin. "But be careful what you wish for."

A HOUR LATER, SADE stuffed a powdered-sugar coated beignet in her mouth and watched the multitude of people either strolling past on the sidewalk or waiting in line for a table at the Café Du Monde. A humorist once quipped that if one sat there long enough, the whole world would pass by. On a day like today, Sade could believe it. It was Saturday and the tourists swarmed Jackson Square and nearby environs. Local artists displayed their wares on the iron fence surrounding the park. At the other end of the square, psychics gathered in front of St. Louis Cathedral and the Cabildo. She didn't need her fortune told to know she needed another cup of café au lait.

A waiter had just delivered two cups—better to grab refills while she had the chance—when the crowd parted. Sade watched with jaded interest, waiting to see who appeared. Her money was on Nikos Constantine. She was close. His lap dragon, Stavros, approached her table. Sade didn't like Stavros. She figured the feeling was mutual.

"Agent Marquis."

"Stavros."

He pulled out a chair and sat without asking. The waiter appeared immediately. Eying the sugary confection and thick-with-cream coffee, the dragon grimaced but ordered the same as what Sade had.

She didn't wait for him to start the conversation. "What do you want?"

"Justice."

"Justice? For Aleta? Or for the Clan?" Sade had taken a quick course on dragon culture in the past twenty-four hours. This visit had nothing to do with the dead girl and everything to do with the injured pride of an overbearing alpha hotel of a dragon enforcer who believed he had the right to do whatever the hell he pleased. In the dragon realm? Maybe. On her turf? Not gonna happen.

"The Drakon requests your presence tonight."

"Requests? That doesn't sound like Nikos Constantine. Ordering me? Yeah. That I believe. Tell him no thanks."

Stavros's silvery eyes slitted and his mouth thinned. He looked far more reptilian than a man should. Rather than lash out at her, he swallowed. Hard. She hoped he bit his tongue until it was bloody.

"Your boss must have you on a short leash."

She leaned toward him and her eyes glittered, reminding Stavros of the emeralds the Drakon wore at his cuffs. The reason this human intrigued Nikos escaped Stavros. He was only here to ensure her compliance. He didn't want to play his trump card if he didn't have to do so.

"Unlike yours, who should muzzle you." The words were out before he could stop them.

Sade blinked and then looked left-right-left in shifty-eyed succession. "Wow. Nice comeback. I'm impressed." Which was the truth. She was impressed. Maybe Stavros wasn't the lap dragon she'd taken him for. "Care to explain why you're really here?"

Despite his lack of a sweet tooth, Stavros bit into the beignet, avoiding the cascade of powdered sugar threatening to coat his dark suit. He would have preferred the fried bread plain. He chewed and swallowed then drained his cup of the café au lait, again preferring it black and unsweetened. As the waiter appeared, he ordered a straight coffee and proceeded to polish off the remaining two beignets on his plate. He was curious how long the FBI agent would wait. Turned out she was a better hunter than he anticipated. He broke the silence.

"I am here because the Drakon of the Kholkikos Clan sent me to find you."

"Because he requests my presence tonight."

"Yes."

Sade picked up her second beignet and shook the majority of the sugar coating it onto the plate. Her lips surrounded the tip of the pastry and she didn't quite suck it before sinking her teeth into it and tearing off a bite. She watched Stavros watch her. His nostrils flared and his eyes widened and when the tip of his tongue appeared Sade couldn't hold back a snort. The dragon jerked as if she'd slapped him and straightened in his chair.

"Jeez. You magicks are so easy."

Stavros glared and shoved to his feet. "We are done here. Present yourself to the Drakon tonight."

"Or what?"

He placed his palms on the table and leaned close to Sade. "I do not believe you wish to discover the answer to that question, Agent Marquis."

CHAPTER SEVENTEEN
ALLY, ALLY OXEN FREE

CALEB HAD ANOTHER HOT DATE with Dr. Toni Allison, which left Sade on her own for the evening. Since her run-in with Stavros at Café Du Monde, her day hadn't improved. She'd caught no hint of Ariel anywhere despite tugging on a lot of strings and offering a lot of favors—something one didn't hand out like candy to a magick—to get news of his whereabouts. She'd gotten zero. Zilch. Nada.

Her stomach growled and the same two older ladies she'd been stuck in the elevator with before glared at her. The stairs took on whole new appeal but a ding and the doors sliding open precluded her escape. She allowed the older tourists to step into the elevator first then she followed.

On the first floor, she cleared the lobby before they did. She planned on a thick, juicy burger, fries, and beer at Déjà Vu. Lots of beer. Loud music. A game on the big screen. A chance to unwind and maybe put the case in prospective.

Sade pushed through the front doors of the Chateau LeMoyne and turned left. She could see the corner building housing the restaurant bar down the block. The place was familiar and with the weird week she'd had, it was time to join the gods in a drink. Her mouth watered and she could almost taste the Bleu Cheese Burger she planned to order.

Then the luxury SUV with blacked-out windows pulled up to the curb next to her and stopped. Her hand automatically reached for her weapon. She might be off duty but she never went unarmed. The back door swung open. Sade tensed.

"You do not follow instructions, Sade."

She couldn't decide if Nikos sounded amused or put out. Not that she cared. "Yeah, I have this thing about authority, Mr. Constantine."

"Nikos."

"Agent Marquis."

"Must we do this dance again?"

"Yeah. Because it's only business between us, Mr. Constantine." Sade resisted the urge to smooth the hair on her arms ruffled by the swell of magic leaking from the SUV. She'd pissed him off. Again. That made her smile.

"Get in the car, Sade."

"I don't think so." She turned to leave and stopped dead in her tracks at his next utterance.

"Do you want to see the fae alive again?"

Drawing on every resource she had, she smoothed her features before turning back to the SUV and tilting her head so she could see the dragon enforcer seated inside. "What the fuck does that mean?"

"What do you think it means, Sade? I know you have a relationship with the King's Seducer. I know you have been protecting him. If you wish to continue doing so, you will get in. If not, then I will deal with the murderer in my own way."

Sade went cold as the blood drained from her face. Her fingers convulsively closed around the butt of her pistol. She couldn't think for a minute, couldn't react. She wanted only to pull her weapon and shred the dragon's heart. If he had hurt Ariel in any way...

"What do you want?"

"I want you to get in the car, Sade. I want you to share dinner with me. I want to talk with you. To get to know you."

"So you blackmail me?"

"Not at all. The King's Seducer killed something that belonged to me. I am within my rights to end his life."

Without thinking through the consequences of her actions, Sade launched her body into the backseat. Her fist connected soundly with the dragon's jaw before Stavros caught her from behind. He slammed her head into the center console, which wasn't as padded as advertised. Stars danced before her eyes.

Stunned, Sade wasn't sure what happened next other than Stavros no longer had a hold of her, and angry words in something she thought might be Greek flew over her head like heat-seeking missiles. The stars still did their cosmic dance and her hair lifted as magic spiked in the confined space. A hand cupped her cheek with utmost care even as the argument raged around her.

Bile churned in her stomach and she threw up a little in her mouth. She forced her eyes to remain open against the concussion she knew she had. Fuck but her head hurt.

"Sade?" The voice saying her name caressed her as soft as the finest velvet.

"Fuck." There. Her mouth worked. Her brain could form a sentence. Sort of.

That voice rumbled in an amused chuckle. "I think you will survive but we will return to the hotel to have my physician make sure."

"No."

"What did you say?"

"No. Hell no." Her lips felt swollen and didn't want to form the words her brain kept sending. Going anywhere with Nikos Constantine was a very bad idea. Capitalize that and add a trademark.

"Drive, Xan."

Arms held her and her head found a place to rest against a rock hard shoulder. The stars stopped their manic spin but didn't go away, though they grew less distinct against the black curtain of her eyelids. She needed to open them. Concussion. Bad idea to sleep. Dragons. Dragons who had Ariel and planned to execute him.

She bolted upright, or tried. She only managed to bang the side of her head against the backseat window. Nikos had her wrapped up as neat as a birthday present, his arms the ribbons holding her immobile.

"Fuck."

"You keep saying that, Sade. It is a crude word but if that is what you wish, we can skip dinner and go straight to my bed."

"Fuck, no." She pushed at his chest and squirmed. "Gawddammit. Let me go."

"No."

The SUV rolled to a smooth stop and a familiar face in a green coat opened the door. "Welcome back, Mr. Constantine. Do you require assistance?"

"No thank you, Charles. I have Ms. Marquis well in hand."

"The hell—"

"Desist, Sade. I want the royal physician to look at your injury and then I want to talk. That is all."

Her head pounded like a tympani drum keeping time with her pulse. When she tried to focus her eyes, her vision was all wonky and she'd lay odds she wouldn't be able to stand and walk at the same time. She was at the dragon's mercy with no backup.

Once on the sidewalk in front of the Monteleone, she managed to stay upright long enough to notice Stavros was nowhere to be found. Before she could protest, Nikos swept her into his arms and carried her inside, up the short flight of steps to the lobby, and around the corner to the elevators. Within minutes, she was seated on a couch in the suite where she'd first interviewed Nikos.

The dragon stood off to the side talking in hushed tones with a man who appeared older. Sade still had enough wits to know the persona was simply a glamour assumed by the second dragon. He approached her looking all solicitous and serious.

"Miss Marquis, I am Dr. Theo."

"Agent."

"Beg pardon?"

"I'm not a miss. I'm an FBI agent."

A faint smile teased his lips. "It is a good sign that your attitude remains."

"I don't have an attitude."

The guffaw exploded from his mouth before Nikos could contain it. His silvery blue eyes twinkled, reminding Sade of moonlight on the ocean. She must be getting better. Maybe she didn't have a concussion. She blinked.

"Stop that."

"Stop what, Sade."

"Agent Mar—"

"This is beyond tiresome, Sade. Need I remind you what is at stake?"

Oh, yeah. Here there be dragons and this one was meaner than a snake. Sade needed to remember that. He looked away and when he faced her again, he'd shuttered his expression.

The woman was positively infuriating. Nikos had never had such trouble before. While she fired his temper, she also piqued his curiosity in ways he'd not experienced before. For a being as old as he was, the novelty of the situation drew him like a moth to flame.

A soft knock on the door attracted his attention and a moment later, Xan entered and offered a brief nod before withdrawing. Stavros had been returned to the dragon realm. Nikos would have to deal with him eventually. That his lieutenant had put him in this position disturbed him. On one side of the coin, Stavros acted on instinct—protecting Nikos when Sade attacked. But on the other, Nikos had guaranteed Sade's safety and since she was only human, she would not have been able to hurt him.

His temper flared as he remembered her reaction. The damned fae meant something special to her. That the King's Seducer might have tasted Sade's passion first was worse than a grain of sand irritating an oyster. Nikos would not form a pearl to smooth his aggravation. He would simply kill his competition and be done with it.

Watching the doctor work on Sade's wound—her forehead had been cut when Stavros slammed her into the console—Nikos came to an abrupt realization. If he killed the fae and Sade truly cared, then any hope for his suit with her would die as well. She was a woman of deep passions—and that included her loyalty—misplaced though it might be.

Nikos had already tried magic. He'd tried trickery. Perhaps it was time to try compassion. The emotion was an unfamiliar one and tasted almost bitter on his tongue. But the prize was worth his lenience. She had promised justice for Aleta. And what better way than to have her mete out the punishment. He smiled and called for Xan.

CHAPTER EIGHTEEN
RESISTANCE

SADE FIDGETED IN HER PADDED CHAIR. She hated formal dining—it brought back the worst memories of growing up in the Dallas mansion belonging to Mathias. Two hours ago, she wanted nothing more than a Déjà Vu burger topped with bleu cheese, fries, and a beer. Or three. And now here she was on the top terrace of the Hotel Monteleone, overlooking the pool and the skyline of New Orleans, staring at more forks, knives, and spoons than any ten people needed in order to eat a meal.

The waiter had already removed the several wine glasses at her place setting. Why she needed a glass for each type of wine served with an eight-course meal made about as much sense as all that silverware. Not that it mattered tonight. No alcohol for her for at least forty-eight hours and that truly sucked. The judicious use of an icepack brought the swelling down on her forehead and a bandage closed the small cut. She hoped Stavros was rotting in some dragon hell at the moment.

Sade winced and took back the thought. Ariel just might be in the cell next to Stavros. She eyed Nikos suspiciously. Luckily, his back was turned so he didn't see the narrowed, stink-eye look, snarled curl of lips, and general distrust she aimed his direction. When he glanced over his shoulder, a frown furrowing his forehead, she was all sweetness and smiles.

"Ariel, you so owe me, you asshole." She muttered the promise under her breath.

Nikos finished his telephone conversation and returned to the table. As he settled into the chair across from her, the waiter appeared to serve the first course. Soup. Cold soup. This was going to be a freaking long evening. She watched the dragon spoon the viscous liquid into his mouth with utmost elegance. The damn man did have meticulous manners. In some ways, he reminded her of her godfather, Mathias. That wasn't necessarily a favorable comparison.

"You do not like the soup?"

"It's fine." She dipped her spoon into the thick concoction and pretended to take a sip. Soup was supposed to be hot. And filled with noodles and meat and onions. Not pureed cucumbers and Greek yogurt.

A second later, the waiter whisked her bowl away and a seafood cocktail appeared. She grabbed the little "Poseidon's trident fork" next to her plate. Stabbing the first shrimp, she dragged it through red sauce and ate. In short order, the oysters and crabmeat disappeared between her lips. A plated salad appeared next. Rabbit food, but better than nothing. She nibbled and waved away the sorbet that followed. She didn't need to cleanse her palate. When a thick filet mignon appeared, she pounced on it like a starving carnivore.

Nikos simply leaned back in his chair and watched—fascinated and horrified both. How did this woman, who appeared so elegant on the surface, turn into such a social beast? Had Mathias simply left her to her own devices as a child? He pretended her disregard of his efforts to entertain her didn't affect him. After all, she was only human—and one who'd received a head injury earlier in the evening.

"You're staring."

"Do you find it rude?"

She paused, a large bite of rare steak poised on her fork. "No."

Her answer surprised him and as she nibbled the meat off the utensil and into her mouth, he found his own mouth too dry to speak. Her eyelids lowered, her expression relaxed, and her jaw flexed slightly. She savored the flavor of the meat like a sommelier tasting a rare vintage wine. Was it that simple? Could it be that the way to Sade's heart was through a piece of aged beef?

Sade chewed and swallowed. Her eyelids drifted up and she met his gaze. "You aren't eating? Not hungry?"

Now Niko swallowed. He was hungry all right. Hungry for this human woman who was such a contradiction. "I shall join you for...dessert." He was all but licking his lips thinking about what he would choose for dessert—Sade Marquis stretched across his bed with her legs spread wide for him.

He recognized the tide of magic at the same moment Sade did. He met an inhuman screech with a roar. Sade met it with silence and a drawn Beretta. The lights went out. In the hotel. In the Quarter. In New Orleans.

"What the fuck?"

"Stay down, Sade."

His dragon vision kicked in. He could see her crouched next to her chair, weapon in hand. The waiter appeared from the service entrance, flashlight in hand. "I'm sorry, sir. Seems there's been—"

The man never finished his explanation. Ear-splitting screeches echoed around them followed by a near-silent swoosh. One moment, the waiter stood near the door. The next, only his shoes—with something bloody still in them—remained.

"What the holyshitandpissfuckaduck gawddammitalltohell sonavabitch is that?"

Another cry, another whoosh, and the table next to Sade crashed onto its side. She scrabbled backwards looking for something to hide under. Whatever the fuck this was, it was way beyond her pay grade and experience. Which meant this was a *really* bad nasty.

Nikos roared another challenge to the dark sky. Something blurred the air between them. When she could see plainly again, the dragon sported four deep gashes across his chest and his designer jacket hung in shreds from his shoulders.

"Holy hell, Nikos! Are you okay?" Sade stood and took three steps toward him before the air stilled around her and hot breath lifted the hair covering her neck.

Time slowed. That wasn't possible because Sade was immune to magic, thanks to the wards and marks placed upon her in infancy by Mathias and Oberon. But it did—like a slow motion film. She turned, raising her pistol. The creature facing her triggered Sade's gag reflex. Red eyes burning with hatred, rotted teeth and breath that stank of sulfur and dead bodies, with skin sloughing off bone in ribbons. She swallowed the bile surging up to choke her and squeezed the trigger.

One. Two. Six. Seven. Eleven. Fifteen. Something in her arsenal of bullets worked—cold iron, silver, high explosive, steel, copper, a combination of all—because the creature exploded. Dry ash drifted down, coating everything.

"What the fuck?" Sade thought she asked the question out loud but she wasn't positive. Lights flickered but her vision darkened on the edges. And then her eyes rolled back in her head.

With his palm flat between her shoulder blades, Nikos forced Sade's head between her knees. "Breathe, Sade. In through your nose, out through your mouth."

She didn't bother retorting, preferring to save her breath for actual breathing.

Nikos resisted the urge to break something. This was not the romantic evening he'd planned. A magnificent dinner on the terrace. Fine wines. The subtle dominance games he so enjoyed. The evening had started out a debacle and was now an unmitigated disaster.

His fingers tingled from her panic—as big an aphrodisiac for a predator as having her naked in his bed. He rubbed her back, moving the rich silk of her hair away so he could gently knead her neck. Her breathing back under control, Sade pushed against his hand to sit up. He allowed her to do so.

Color flushed her pallid cheeks as her brazen attitude returned. That's what drew him. He appreciated her aggressiveness, so unlike the docile women in the dragon realm. He studied her and their situation. Only a fool would attack a dragon in his lair.

"What the hell was that thing?" Sade almost sounded normal.

"Now there's the question."

"Who the hell sent it?"

"Who indeed." His eyes narrowed to slits, their pale blue shading to silver before hardening to titanium.

"Did I kill it?"

"No."

Sade gained her feet and spun in a slow circle as she studied the sky. "Will it come back?"

"Are you afraid?"

She lowered her face slightly to stare at him. "Damn straight I am. But that doesn't mean I won't kill it the next time it shows up."

"You will have to beat me to it."

"That can be arranged."

And there she was—the indomitable human with flashing emerald eyes. She would be his. Sooner or later.

CHAPTER NINETEEN
IT GETS WORSE

A HANDFUL OF LOCAL COPS, assisted by several dragons, corralled the hotel staff. Caleb left his date, assistant ME Toni Allison to her work, what little there was, and joined Sade. She did her best to describe the creature that had attacked them. When she finished, she stared at Caleb, waiting for his analysis.

He stared out over the restored lights of the Quarter, gathering his thoughts. "It couldn't have been a *Nachthexen*. The last one of those died in Moscow ten years ago."

"A what?" Sade didn't even try to pronounce the word.

"Night witch," Caleb explained. "It's Russian."

Sade watched Toni kneeling beside the pair of once-polished shoes now covered in gore. Tattered bones and flesh stuck up at odd angles. "It took a man off at the knees. In one pass." She inhaled through her mouth to avoid the smell, held it for almost a minute then exhaled through her nose. She felt in charge now. And pissed. When she got hit with an adrenaline rush, there was no such thing as flight. She was fight all the way.

Striding toward Nikos, she didn't wait for him to turn and intercept her. She grabbed his arm and jerked—which was sort of like tugging on Superman's cape. Nothing happened. She stepped between him and his shadow dragon, Xan.

She stood toe-to-toe with Nikos, chin jutted, eyes blazing. "Where the fuck is Ariel?"

Caleb was two steps too slow. He didn't know who to grab first so he protected Sade's back, eying the guard, his hand curled into a partial change.

"He is secure." Nikos answered her, obviously distracted.

"That's not what I asked, asshole. Where is he?"

"He is in a room made of cold iron."

"Then this..." She waved one hand in a confused circle. "This...thing isn't his magic. Iron blocks his magic."

Nikos opened his mouth to retort before clamping his jaw. He didn't want to admit it, but he replied, "You are correct."

"How long have you had him?"

"Since yesterday."

"So he had no clue you were blackmailing me into dinner tonight, nor the location? There's no way he could have conjured this thing beforehand. He didn't do this."

Nikos pondered her assertions and concluded she was correct once again. Other forces were at work here, though that did not preclude the fae's guilt regarding Aleta's murder.

When the dragon didn't reply, Sade rocked up on her toes. "Release him. Immediately."

"He is still the last person to have seen Aleta."

"The hell you say. She returned from her date with him. Slept in her own fucking bed and was in the gawddammed park with her charges. Your fucking bodyguards were the last ones to see her. Why aren't they in chains?"

Anger surged inside him, making his fingers tingle with the urge to strangle this upstart human.

"Tell me where he is. I'll arrange to have him transported to NOPD for questioning." Caleb's measured voice cut through the tension.

Nikos breathed. Sade breathed. Caleb let out a soft *whew*. Sade's phone broke the rest of the spell when it played AC-DC's "Hard as a Rock." She answered it without preamble.

"Roman!"

"Are you safe?"

"Yeah. What the fuck, Roman? Do you know what that thing was?"

"I'm tracking it at the moment."

"Can you take it?"

His rumbling laughter reverberated from the cell phone. "I am a gargoyle, Sade."

"You didn't answer me. What the fuck is it?"

"A *bansidhe*. Where is Ariel?"

"A *bansidhe*? I thought those were just death harbingers. And what's Ariel got to do with it?"

"It takes a high-ranking fae to summon a *bansidhe* and control her, Sade."

"It wasn't Ariel."

"Sade—"

"Don't Sade me, Roman. The fucking dragons have had Ariel confined in cold iron since yesterday. There's no way it was him."

"Then we have larger problems."

"No shit, Sherlock. Let me know if you find that bitch. I want a piece of her."

"The *bansidhe* will be dealt with, Sade, but not by you or any other human."

"She killed a human—"

"I am aware of that. She is too dangerous for human authorities, including you. I want no more human blood spilled."

Sade chewed on the insides of her cheeks before finally agreeing. "Just be careful, okay?"

"Always, Lady Sade."

Roman broke the connection and Sade stared at the magicks surrounding her. "Well...alrighty then."

Sade did her best to ignore the beads of sweat dotting Ariel's forehead but the red welts circling his wrists made her cringe. Cold iron and fae skin created an excruciating combination. "Ariel?"

He opened pain-glazed eyes and fixed them on her. "I must have really pissed you off this time." His mouth twisted into his arrogant grin despite the agony shuddering through his body.

"Oh, Ari. What the hell have you gotten mixed up in?"

His eyelids drooped as if all the energy had leeched out of him. "I didn't do this, Sade."

She touched his arm and he winced. Jerking her hand back, she glared at the two-way mirror on the far wall. "Get your ass in here and unshackle him." When no one appeared within five heartbeats, she unholstered her Beretta and aimed at the window. "You have five seconds. One. Two."

The door flew open, banging against the wall. A uniformed NOPD cop loomed over her. Before he could react, she'd snatched his keys and freed the fae. When the officer opened his mouth, she held up one finger. "I vouch for him. He's not going anywhere."

A loud growl echoed behind the glass and moments later, all the human cops cleared out, leaving Caleb alone in the hidden room to monitor her interrogation. What she needed to know was not for mundane ears. She shooed the big cop out and shut the door.

"Better?"

"Yeah, thanks."

"Talk to me, Ariel. Who has it out for you?" He refused to look at her. "Well, fuck. It's not Oberon, is it?"

That got his attention. "No."

"Then who?"

"Titania's whore."

"Whoa. Queen Titty-fae has a whore?" The look on Ariel's face spoke volumes. "Well, duh. Of course she does. King's Seducer, Queen's Whore. So Titania has it out for you?"

Ariel looked a little green around the gills. "No. Tempe declared this war all on her own."

"Why you?"

114

"Because she wants to switch sides. If the psychotic bitch had her way, she'd be Oberon's consort, not Titania."

"Does Titania know this?"

"She will. A fae doesn't summon a *bansidhe* under the Court's nose and go unnoticed."

Sade scrunched her lips and nose in an expression of thought. Ariel closed his eyes, doing his best not to show the shudders of pain still rocking through his body.

"Ariel?"

He cracked open one eyelid. The look of compassion on Sade's face would have brought him to his knees if he'd had the strength to stand.

"What are you not telling me?"

Ari lifted one shoulder in a negligent shrug. "This isn't the first time I've had a run in with her."

Sade stared, silent, though her expression demanded he explain.

"She caught me once." The memory strengthened the shakes consuming his body.

"Ah hell, Ari. What the fuck did she do to you?"

"The easier question to answer would be what didn't she do." He managed to stand despite the tremors. He fumbled with his silver belt buckle waiting for one of Sade's patented smart remarks. She remained silent, watching him, her eyes liquid emeralds.

He finally managed to dislodge belt and buttons and his jeans dipped low over one hip. "You know we heal, right? Without scars?"

Sade nodded, her concern plowing furrows in her forehead.

Ari pushed down his jeans, revealing a tawny treasure trail headed lower. Until it abruptly stopped, bisected by an ugly scar and something that resembled a seal of some sort. Or a brand.

Her chest ached and Sade couldn't breathe. Holy crap! What would disfigure a fae like that? And what sort of excruciating pain was involved? She couldn't guess. Didn't want to. She turned away and flicked her fingers across her cheek to stop the tear trickling down it. She tried to speak but couldn't form a word, only a croak. She cleared her throat. Tried again.

"Well fuck, Ari."

"That wasn't really the worst of it."

"Seriously? What could be worse than that?"

"She's my sister."

CHAPTER TWENTY
DEAD OR ALIVE

ONCE AGAIN, SADE PACED the confines of the Legate's office. "How the hell do I track down a rogue fae?" She turned just in time to catch the looks Roman and Caleb exchanged. "No. Forget it, Roman."

"You do not even know what I am thinking, Sade."

"Yes, I do. You want to let the Seelie Court catch her and handle it. She did the crimes in the human realm. We have to be the ones to deal with her." She held up a warning finger. "Humans have to make a stand. They have to understand that there are laws and justice and that the Dark Days are over."

Her shoulders slumped a little. "Don't you see, Roman? Everyone has to play by the rules or the indiscriminate killing won't stop. You know better than anyone that humans react from fear. And what we fear, we kill." Straightening, Sade tilted her chin so she could look directly into the gargoyle's eyes.

"I don't want to bury any of you."

And there it was, Roman thought. The reason she held the position she did in the FBI. The reason she fought so fiercely and loyally. She cared. About magicks. About humans. About law and justice and mercy.

"You should have been a gargoyle, Lady Sade."

A gigglesnort burst from her. "Damn, Romo. I think I hurt something." She didn't sit but she stopped pacing. "Do you know where they took Ariel?"

Caleb glanced up from the text he was typing into his phone. "Oberon secured him in the Summer Palace. No one knows he's there beyond a few trusted guards and Oberon's private physician." He read something in her expression and added, "He'll be okay, Sade. Oberon's beyond pissed and Titania's reaction went off the Richter scale. At this point, it's just a matter of who gets to Tempe first."

"Then I intend to be first. How do we draw her out?"

Caleb and Roman exchanged another of their shadowed looks before Roman spoke. "We don't, Sade. Or more specifically, *you* don't."

"Fine. Don't help me." She pivoted on her heel, marched to the door, and disappeared through it.

"Well, that's a fine kettle of fish you've gotten us into, Stanley." Caleb managed a decent impression of Oliver Hardy. "I told you not to give her an ultimatum like that."

Roman swiveled to watch out the window. A few moments later, Sade appeared on the street below. Her long-legged stride was unmistakable as she headed toward Jackson Square. "Then you'd best follow her before Tempe decides to take out the one woman Ariel has obsessed over for the last ten years."

Feral red lights flickered deep in Caleb's eyes. "You provoked her on purpose? Why?"

"Because it's so easy to do?" Roman effortlessly caught the marble bust Caleb launched at his head. "Tempe will go after Sade now that she knows how much Ariel cares."

"You can't use Sade as bait."

"I am always amazed at how easily you underestimate her, Caleb. Why do you think she called that press conference this morning?"

Caleb's mouth opened and closed a few times before he spit out one word. "Bitch."

"Indeed. She set herself up as a target. And it is now up to us to make sure her bravado does not backfire."

Caleb caught up to Sade in front of St. Louis Cathedral. The psychics and fortune tellers who hawked their wares were folding up for the night. Gloaming filled the square, smudging sharp edges with shadows. He glanced toward a girl huddled under a colorful umbrella at the end of the row. With her nose stuck in a romance novel, she seemed oblivious to the creeping darkness. A hand-lettered placard decorated with flowers and vines proclaimed, "Tarot by Desi." The air shimmered around her and Caleb almost stopped but he had more pressing things to do—like stay with Sade before Tempe Daoine put in appearance. He would have to investigate the girl's magic another time.

"Where we headed?"

"Back to the hotel."

"We gonna stop and eat first?"

Sade came to a halt. And considered. "Breakfast *was* a long time ago."

By mutual consent, they headed directly to Déjà Vu. Sade was finally going to get that Bleu Cheese burger, fries, and duty—or concussion—be damned, she was going to drink a beer. On tap.

Side-by-side, they dodged the Sunday evening foot traffic. Twilight turned to dark and decorative gaslights flared on. Noise and neon spilled from the open door of the restaurant and bar when they arrived at the corner of Conti and Dauphine.

The bartender waved as they ducked through the entrance. Sade yelled over the sound spitting from hidden speakers, "A Magic Hat and a Guinness!" Jax was wiping down her booth and ice waters were lined up awaiting her arrival.

"I swear you're part camel, cher," the waiter said. "You need menus?"

They ordered sans menus and slid into the booth as the bartender arrived with their beer. Due to the positioning of the speakers, this corner of the room was quieter—another reason Sade preferred sitting there.

"You know she's going to come after you."

"Duh."

"Dammit, Sade."

"Ooh, look who's cussing now." She leaned back and took a long draw of beer. "I need to figure out how to get her isolated so there's no collateral damage."

"Darlin', that collateral damage includes you."

Sade lifted a hand in a negligent wave. "Not gonna happen. I know who and what I'm looking for now. Roman took care of the *bansidhe* and with the Seelie Court on notice, there's no way that psychotic bitch can summon another one."

"I don't think you understand, Sade. The amount of dark magic needed to do what Tempe has done is…" He paused, at a loss for words. "Look, bottom line. You can't take any chances with her. She's killed a werewolf, a fae, a vampire, and a dragon."

"A female werewolf who was a socialite. No offense, Caleb. But Victoria Smith wasn't exactly a street fighter. And the vampire was a judge. The dragon a nanny. The only one she might have had trouble with is the fae. Alvin had been a royal guard but I've seen them all up close. They're lazy. If he wasn't expecting an attack—"

Jax arrived with their plates and more water. "Do you even realize how much water you drink?" He fisted his hands on his hips and offered her a fish-eyed stare. "There is such a thing as water poisoning, cher. Just sayin'."

Sade laughed and toasted him with one of the fresh glasses. "I promise to drink more beer. Okay?"

The waiter winked and wandered off to clean a table just vacated by a group of locals.

Caleb wolfed down his burger then devoured his fries. Sade ate more sedately. She'd just swallowed a bite and was already cussing before the second note of her ring tone played "Cops." "Dammit, if there's another dead magick I'm going postal on the fucking fae court." She answered and listened.

"Are you shittin' me? Fucking zombies? Is that even possible?" She glanced at Caleb. "No. I'm not asking you, Detective, I'm asking my partner."

Caleb shrugged as he slid out of the booth and dropped money on the table. Sade grabbed her burger and headed for the door, still talking on the phone. "Okay, okay. Just keep the gates closed. We're three blocks away."

Sade hated to eat and run. She hated eating *while* running even more but she managed to chow down the rest of her burger without choking. They could hear screaming and yelling before they turned the corner onto Basin Street and jogged across the lanes of traffic and wide median. NOPD officers tried their best to sort out the snarled traffic. People milled around the narrow gate leading into the cemetery, snapping pictures and making Vine videos with their smartphones.

Caleb took the lead and the crowd parted at his growled commands. Sade followed in his wake. A knot of harried cops welcomed them with relief. One of the bystanders tried to climb the wall surrounding the cemetery with the help of two buddies. Caleb ripped him down and showed teeth.

Sade put her fingers in her mouth and whistled shrilly. "That's it. Anyone not carrying a badge who's still standing here in five seconds is going to jail."

A big man surged forward. "Oh yeah, what grounds—" The mouthy guy found himself face down on the pavement, arms twisted behind his back as Sade very efficiently cuffed him. She hauled him back to his feet and shoved him toward the nearest police car.

"Interfering with a federal investigation, asshole. Three...two..."

The crowd scattered like cockroaches under a spotlight. The local cops took a collective breath. Sade found the one wearing lieutenant's bars. The man looked like he'd gone twelve rounds with an MMA fighter.

"Are you sure we're dealing with zombies?"

The cop shuddered. "Oh yeah."

"I didn't think zombies actually—"

An uncanny wail rose and fell like an air raid siren. Everyone spun to stare through the wrought iron gate. Sade cut her eyes to Caleb with a "Well?" expression on her face.

"Technically, they don't exist but working very strong black magic can create them."

"So how do we kill them?"

Caleb looked troubled. "Not sure. I'd guess fire."

"Great. Who has a stock of flamethrowers?"

The cops chuckled nervously.

"Can you at least check with the National Guard or something?" Sade prompted.

"Good idea. Yeah. I'll get right on that." The lieutenant took off at a dead run for the nearest squad car. The other officers backed away from the gate.

Caleb grinned, winked, and in his best Paul Newman voice said, "Well, Sundance. It's just you and me, kid."

"So what's the plan, Butch?"

"Move in slowly, check out everything. The thing to remember—"

"Don't tell me how to rob a bank. I know how to rob a bank." Sade grinned and tried to remember the last time they'd quoted movie lines to each other. Way too long for sure. She pulled her Beretta and pushed open the gate, which grated against the concrete path beneath it.

Caleb ducked through, using the first tomb on his left as cover. Sade followed, fading to the right. They advanced through the alleys of the dead taking turns covering each other. The shuffling dead had apparently gone to ground. Caleb disappeared around the corner of a mausoleum. Sade turned to check their back trail. The zombies were smarter than they looked. They'd circled around to cut Sade and Caleb off from the only exit.

"Who *are* those guys?"

"Shut up, Caleb. This is serious."

"It always is. C'mon." He trotted off, weaving between crypts, without a backward glance to see if she was following.

She counted at least ten zombies before she headed after him. Who the hell had enough bad mojo to raise ten zombies? This Tempe bitch was really starting to piss her off. It was bad enough to torture Ariel and murder a bunch of innocent magicks, but she'd also killed a human. Not by her own hands but by her magic. That was enough for Sade to act as judge, jury, and executioner.

The handheld radio she'd taken from one of the New Orleans' cops crackled. "Agent Marquis?"

"Do you have those flamethrowers yet?"

"Uhm…no, ma'am. The LT is checking with the World War Two museum to see if they have any."

"Seriously? Call the fire department. Maybe we can drown the suckers."

Caleb had stopped, his shoulder pressed against a white-washed tomb while he scratched Xs on it. "What the fuck, Caleb?"

He pointed to the name plaque. "I'm not taking any chances. Gotta make an X three times. For luck. Or so she doesn't curse you. Or something."

Sade rolled her eyes. "So have you gotten a good whiff?"

"You mean of the rotten, putrefied bodies?" He rolled his eyes in mimic of her action. "Yeah. It's Tempe all right. Her magic is all over 'em."

"Then it's time to get to work, *kemosabe*." She peered around the corner of Marie Laveau's tomb. "Sorta wish I smoked about now," she muttered. "And carried a big ol' can of hairspray."

"Nobody makes aerosol spray any more. It's bad for the environment."

She took her eyes off the shuffling horde just long enough to glare at her partner. "Seriously, Caleb?"

The werewolf shrugged. "We'd be better off with a steaming pile of guts. That would distract them long enough for us to get over the wall."

Sade measured the brick and stucco wall surrounding the cemetery with her gaze. They'd have about a forty-yard dash before they got to the base of it, and then they'd have to get over twelve feet of fence. "Easy for you to say. I'm only human."

The ten zombies she originally counted had multiplied. There were at least twenty now, probably more. The creatures hesitated, those in front stopping completely while the ones bringing up the rear shambled into the ones ahead of them. Something stirred the air sending little whirlwinds dancing through the humidity. Heads moved. Faces tilted toward the sky. Sade heard the whisper of leathery wings.

Roman?

She caught a glimpse of the gargoyle as he landed in the midst of the mob. Pandemonium erupted as rotting limbs and heads sailed through the air, splatting against tombs.

"Roman! I need one alive!"

Caleb laughed. "Uhm…Sade? You do realize they're zombies, right?"

"Yeah. That's why I need one a—" She blinked, her eyes cutting from left to right and back to left as she considered the implications and then she stared at Caleb. "Oh. Duh." She peeked around the tomb again. "Roman! I need a dead one! It's evidence."

CHAPTER TWENTY-ONE
TEMPE IN A TEAPOT

SADE AND CALEB WATCHED the fire department douse the last embers of the small bonfire burning in the corner of the cemetery. Roman had departed with two of the zombies in tow to put them on ice at the M.E.'s office. The remains of the rest smoldered under the spray from the fire hose. A voodoo priestess had been summoned to keep the pesky creatures under control if the mojo Roman had zapped them with wore off while they were in the morgue.

"Do you have the scent?"

Caleb's nostrils flared and his tongue all but hung from the side of his mouth in a wolfish pant. "Oh yeah. Her magic is all over the place. I should have picked up on it when we found Alvin here but when Ariel showed up so soon I figured it was his scent."

"Yeah. That's the way she planned it. She set him up for every blasted one of these, Caleb. Makes me glad I'm an only child." When he stiffened, Sade glanced at him. "You don't count."

"Obviously."

She bumped his shoulder with hers. "You don't count because you aren't my brother through a shared DNA. I picked you to be family. That's different."

Caleb relaxed and bumped her back. "Are you ready to go hunting?"

"Yeah. Let's get the bitch and show her why it's a bad idea to go messing around in our territory."

They fell into a comfortable rhythm born of their years together. Caleb led, Sade protected his back. Until he stopped in front of a nightclub on the far side of Bourbon Street with the unlikely name of *Hot Bloods*. The doorman was big enough to be a troll but he looked both human and smarter than a stump.

"There's a cover charge."

"How much?"

"You get in for five. Twenty bucks for him."

Sade exchanged a look with Caleb. She flicked back her jacket so the gold of her FBI badge caught the neon flashes from the signs in the bar's window. "Naw. I think this gets us a free pass. He has one, too."

The doorman's eyes widened and he cast a worried glance over his shoulder. "Look, we run a clean joint here. We don't want no trouble."

"We're not looking for trouble. We *are*, however, looking for someone and the trail led straight to this club. Here's the deal, you pretend we're not here and we don't tell your boss you let us in. Okay?"

The big guy thought it over. He was still thinking when Sade and Caleb brushed past him and went in. They split up, Caleb going left toward the dance floor. Sade headed the other direction, circling around to the bar. She reached the closest end of it and found an empty spot. She didn't have a chance to prop her hip on the barstool before a kid who looked barely legal swaggered up. He flashed a fangy smile.

"I will feast on your blood. I am the vampire Marceau."

Sade stared—fascinated in a passing-by-a-train-wreck sort of way. Lights strobed in time to throbbing music. Was he doing pelvic thrusts at her? Seriously? As a roving searchlight slashed across his face, he glittered. Glittered for chrissakes! Sade resisted the urge to pound her forehead on the nearest hard surface. Bar top, she quickly amended as the guy stepped closer. He was definitely gyrating his hips à la Elvis and his hard-on couldn't be missed considering the tight pants glued to his skinny hips.

"Is that a sock in your pocket or are you just happy to see me?"

The man stopped as if he'd run into an invisible wall. Sade gazed past his shoulder.

"Well, if it isn't the ice queen herself," the coalescing shadow drawled. "To what do I owe the pleasure?"

"You're slipping, Sebastien." She flicked her gaze toward the man held enthralled by the vampire's power. "Never figured you'd tolerate a poser."

Sebastien sniffed and offered a haughty glare. "How did you know?"

"He glitters. I mean…really? Going for the teenage angst crowd now?"

"You're here. I must be doing something right."

Sade laughed. Hard. But she was dead serious when she said, "I have dead magicks. That's the only reason I'm here. Did you declare open season?"

The vampire's fingertips traced the curve of her cheek. "Only on you. I knew you would come back to me someday, my dear."

"Wrong answer." Sebastien crumpled at her feet following a twist of her hand. She had him by the short hairs and he'd gone to his knees. "Where's the special room, Sebastien?"

He squeaked and swallowed whatever word he was trying to say.

Looming over him, Sade bent from the waist and squeezed harder. "What? I didn't quite catch that. Where do the magicks go to play when they come in, Sebastien? Don't make me hurt you." She eased up the pressure enough that he could speak.

"Go to hell. You can't make me. I don't have to tell you a thing. This is New Orleans and since the Legate died, it's open territory."

She squatted and rocked back on her heels so they were eye-to-eye. "Here's the deal, slick. New Orleans is in Louisiana. Louisiana is in the United States. I'm the agent in charge of the FBI's Magical Activities, Grievances, and

Inhuman Crimes Unit. That gives me jurisdiction over any crime involving a magick anywhere in the whole fucking country." She smirked and added, "And the new Legate? Yeah, I have the feeling you're about get to know him real well."

Even above the pounding music, Caleb's sharp whistle drew her attention. He pointed to a heavily draped wall on the far side of the dance floor. He'd found the entrance to the Little Magicks' Room.

Sade loosened her hand and made a show of wiping her palm on her slacks as she straightened to her full height. The vampire still cowered at her feet. "Don't move, Sebastien. If my suspect isn't in that room, you're going to wake up in the middle of Jackson Square at high noon."

Sebastien gulped but stayed crouched on the floor. Sade headed in Caleb's direction and from the corner of her eye, watched the vampire scurry around the corner of the bar so he could cower behind it. She'd soon find out if he'd alerted the magicks in the room behind the curtain.

She joined Caleb, her hand on the knob of the door. It turned easily. With the ease born of practiced trust, they entered the room, Sade high, Caleb low, weapons drawn. Two vampires looked up from the necks of their humans. Neither human was enthralled. Both were smiling. Sade moved on. Two werewolves danced to the piped-in music. Two male fae sat at the bar, an empty stool between them. They each held a glass and a third glass sweated rings on the wooden surface of the bar.

"Where is she?"

The larger fae's gaze traveled from her face to her chest and lodged there. "She who?"

"Tempe Daoine."

"Never heard of her."

"The Queen's Whore? Really? Nice try, glitter boy." Sade turned a slow circle, her gaze seeking out all the nooks and crannies. She had the attention of everyone in the room now. "Why are you hiding, Tempe? Afraid of li'l ol' me?"

The screech from behind gave Sade just enough time to duck and twist out of reach. The enraged fae flew past, stopped, and whirled.

"You meddling bitch. My brother would be dead now if not for your interference." Tempe's eyes whirled with colors and spittle flew from her mouth as she screamed.

"Yeah, whatever. Tempe Daoine, you're under arrest for the murders of—"

The fae launched at Sade and landed a hard punch to the side of her head. Despite expecting an attack, Sade was slow to react. Stunned by the blow, she landed the floor. Tempe had knocked her on her butt, and her weapon skittered away. Caleb jumped into the fray, only to be ambushed by the second fae. Magic and growls filled the air.

Sade shook her head to clear the fog but before she could push to her feet, Tempe was throwing magic at her. She launched at the fae, hitting Tempe in the solar plexus with her shoulder, knocking the breath out of the other woman. Straddling the bitch, Sade fought to control her long enough to get her cuffed. Tempe shimmered as more magic built in the room.

"Your fucking fae shit doesn't work on me, Tempe. You can thank Oberon for that." She managed to get one handcuff on before the fae threw her off.

Tempe hissed and shook her hand, trying to get the cuffs off without touching them. She scrambled to her feet, breathing hard. Her irises swirled with myriad colors as magic built inside her again. "I am not the weakling my brother is. You will need more than this puny device to hold me."

"Seriously? Who the fuck talks like that?" Sade crabbed backwards, her right hand blindly patting the floor as she attempted to locate her pistol. She barely had time to brace herself before Tempe was on top of her, fists swinging.

The fae's fist connected with Sade's cheekbone and pain burst in her head. Fuck but that hurt. Squirming, Sade managed to plant a foot against Tempe's chest and shoved. Her opponent didn't go far. Fighting magicks was never fair.

Her fingers closed around something cold and metal and it took a moment to realize her weapon was now in her hand. Sade aimed haphazardly and pulled the trigger. The first bullet missed but the second caught Tempe in the chest. Stunned, the fae stared at Sade and then her gaze traveled down to the blood spreading across her sequined bodice.

"You shot me." Tempe sounded like a hurt child and looked shocked that Sade would be so crass as to put a bullet in her.

"Yeah. I did."

"But…" The fae's eyes rolled up in her head and she collapsed to the floor in slow motion.

"That's gonna hurt and leave a mark."

Sade laughed and pretended there wasn't a touch of hysteria to the sound. "You are the master of understatement, Caleb. Get cuffs on her."

"Are you sure you didn't hit anything vital?"

"Pretty sure. But the bullet is iron."

"Did you reload when I wasn't looking?"

Sade winked at him. "I'm always prepared, partner." She surveyed the room. The vamps and their liquid desserts hadn't moved. The werewolves, looking bored, now sat at a table in one corner. The male fae who had attacked Caleb lay bruised, bleeding, and cuffed on the floor. The other fae remained seated at the bar as if he'd been frozen. He tried for nonchalance but failed.

"Should I mention that Oberon is looking for you?"

He blanched and winked out before Sade could slap cuffs on him.

"Damn. Remind me to cuff first, threaten later. Oh, well. He's Uncle Obi-wan's problem now."

The door to the main club banged against the wall. As one, Caleb and Sade swung toward it, weapons aimed and ready. Roman strode in, followed by a man just as tall and broad. Sade relaxed and holstered her weapon.

"You started without me." Roman's voice sounded mild but the reprimand was evident.

Sade bristled, her cheeks flushing with color. She holstered her weapon but kept her palm on the butt while the fingers on her other hand curled into a fist. "We had this discussion, Roman. Or should I call you *Legate* now? This is my case. And she's my prisoner."

"So she is, Sade. I am here to offer assistance only."

"Damn," the second gargoyle murmured as he checked on Tempe. "Who took her down?"

Her gaze raked over the stranger as Sade replied, "That would be me."

"How did a human take down a fae?"

Her Beretta reappeared in her hand as if by magic and she had it aimed at the gargoyle's head. "FYI, the next bullet in this clip contains high explosives."

The gargoyle offered an awed smile. "Clever. I'm Varrick."

"Well, Clever I'm Varrick, what the hell are you doing in my crime scene?"

Roman watched the byplay with interest as he answered. "Varrick is a Sentinel, Sade. I asked him to transport Tempe." Roman folded his arms over his chest, arched one brow, and stared down at her from his impressive height.

"Transport her where?"

"To hospital. Where else?"

"I'll do that."

"How? You have no car, nor do you have any sort of magical capabilities. Unless you hit some significant internal organ, she will recover in hours and then where will you be?" Roman remained poker faced. Mostly.

Sade muttered incomprehensible curses under her breath. The gargoyle was right—as usual. She had to interview all the witnesses and the paperwork from that alone was enough to keep her awake most of the night. Tempe moaned but didn't regain consciousness.

"Okay, fine." She heaved an exaggerated sigh, her first in what would become a very long day. "I still have to fill out a report. In triplicate. Gods but I hate paperwork."

CHAPTER TWENTY-TWO
CAST A SPELL ON ME

SADE HOPED THE DAMNED GODS were bloody well hung over. She stared bleary-eyed at Caleb. He looked not a bit worse for the wear from their adventures, despite going one-on-one with a fae. Jax sailed by and tossed her an ice pack. She snagged it in mid-air, propped her elbow on the table, and leaned her cheek against its cold comfort.

"You should have ducked."

"Shut up, Caleb. She's a fucking fae. The only reason you don't look like me is because you're a werewolf."

Jax appeared with their standard breakfast order. As bad as her head and jaw hurt, Sade considered a bowl of oatmeal instead. The whole side of her face was bruised and swollen but the scent of the bacon alone was enough to change her mind. She thought about it for a moment, weighing each choice. Bacon. Oatmeal. Bacon. Oatmeal. Like anyone would actually make that choice?

For once, no one interrupted them. The TVs in the bar were tuned to the morning sports programs, the volume set low. Locals filtered in from their late night jobs and ordered what would be dinner and drinks based on their internal clocks.

The events last night seemed almost anticlimactic given everything that had happened the past week. Slowly but surely, and after three mugs of coffee, Sade felt like she could open her eyes and face the day. Until her phone rang. She voted to let it go to voice mail as she ignored it.

When Dr. Toni Allison appeared in the doorway, Sade waved her over. Caleb stood up to let Toni slid into the booth beside him. Her breakfast didn't take long to arrive. Sade drank coffee, waiting for Toni to finish eating.

"You look like crap."

"I'll thank you to keep your opinions to yourself, Doc."

"Did you at least get the license number?"

"Har de har har." Sade's phone dinged. She had mail. Voice mail that is. It was Nikos. He wanted to see her in Jackson Square. On Psychic's Row.

The street performer set down his portable karaoke machine and fiddled with the microphone. When he had it adjusted so that no feedback squeals would affect his performance, he launched into an Elvis classic, sounding exactly like the king. That song segued into a Madonna song and he ramped up his antics, much to the audience's appreciation. Applause and money in his jar rewarded his effort. He watched the edge of the crowd gathered around him and smiled at the group skirting past. He fiddled with his machine and the smooth sound of a big band filled the air. A fedora appeared on his head and his face and demeanor morphed into a damn-fine impression of Frank Sinatra. He sang, "That ol' black magic has me in its spell..."

Sade avoided the people watching the singer, even though she had to admit he was pretty good. She headed toward the bench occupied by one person.

The dragon stretched and flexed. If she didn't know better, she'd think this particular dragon was preening. But he wasn't. It was that damn dragon thing resulting from cramming all that magical energy into a human-sized body. If you could call almost seven feet human-sized. She'd at least learned that much about dragons in the past few days.

The only magick in Sade's acquaintance bigger was Roman. In a one-on-one clash, she wasn't sure if she'd bet on the gargoyle or the dragon. And wasn't that a sad commentary on her life?

Her best friends were a werewolf and a gargoyle. The only man trying to get into her pants had been ordered to do so by the fae king, Oberon. Oh, yeah. She'd forgotten. Two men. The second was this freaking dragon. She couldn't figure out his motive and wasn't sure she wanted to know.

Caleb strolled up hand-in-hand with Toni. The assistant ME looked a little despondent if still starry-eyed over her brief affair with the werewolf. Sade had warned the doctor. Caleb was a love-em-and-leave-em kind of wolf. She didn't begrudge them their time together. Much. She wanted to Gibb's slap herself for being so maudlin. Caleb and the doc moved away, watching the street singer and saying their goodbyes.

She plopped down and after a few moments, glanced at the handsome man sitting on the bench beside her—the one tourists openly ogled. This was the problem with hanging around magicks when only human. They were beef tenderloin. She was chopped liver.

At least they'd solved the case. Ariel had been cleared. The real culprit was in the custody of the Council pending a human trial. As much as Sade hated to call in the Council, New Orleans hadn't made provisions for magick prisoners in its jail. She was still a bit shocked that the murderer turned out to be Ariel's sister, Tempe. Just went to show that even the best of families had bad seeds.

She glanced back at Caleb and the doc. They'd stopped kissing and she was listening to her phone. One last quick shared kiss with Caleb before Toni waved. "Duty calls, Marquis. Don't be a stranger. Life is darn sure interesting with you around." She winked at Caleb and sighed deeply as her gaze took in Nikos and Xan. "Yeah. Definitely more interesting."

Sade laughed. Toni would be fine. "Stay out of trouble, Doc."

While she'd hoped for some time off to play tourist in New Orleans, the director's call that morning cut short any hope of a vacation. She and Caleb were headed back to

Washington, DC that afternoon, and straight into another case. Sade closed her eyes and wished for an ice pack. If she rubbed her cheek, it would only hurt worse.

Sweeping his gaze from her head to her toes and back again, Nikos focused on her face. He tamped down his anger that anyone had marred her beauty with physical violence—including his own dragon. The swelling along her jaw and under her eye could not be hidden by the makeup she'd slathered on to cover the bruising. No one touched something of his. Those who had injured Sade would pay.

Sade glanced at Nikos and wondered for a moment what it would be like to sleep with him, to come home at the end of a case—And that's when reality crashed into the fantasy. Nikos was not the type. Like Caleb, like Ariel, like all the magicks, he was a lady-killer—hopefully only in the poetic sense. None of them would ever settle down until the rules of their species forced them to mate. Besides, she didn't want or need the hassle. Magicks were possessive buggers. Deep down, she shied away from the commitment as well. Still, it would be nice to be wanted for longer than a night. Dragging her thoughts away from the despair building inside her, she opened the conversation.

"So what are your plans now?"

"Find a warm body." He licked his lips as his gaze raked her from top to bottom before lingering on her face.

Sade flushed. Dragons radiated heat. That's why she felt so warm. The *only* reason she did. His full, sensuous lips curled into a knowing smile, as if he'd read her previous thoughts—and her current ones. Her fist curled in response and she thumped him in the middle of his chest.

"I'm not food."

He threw back his head and laughter roared out of him, startling the pigeons in the square. "When I eat you, Special Agent Sade Marquis, it will not be for dinner."

"Yeah, in your dreams, dragon breath." She stood and stepped away.

"I'll see you there, darling."

Arrogant man. Dragon. Whatever. Sade pivoted on her toes, prepared to storm away, only to come nose to chest with a rock-hard body—literally. Roman's massive hands gripped her biceps to keep her from falling on her ass—the one not for arrogant dragons, despite the way Nikos ogled it.

"Sade."

"Roman." She looked up until her head cranked back on her neck. Roman was half a foot taller than the dragon and she could feel the animosity swirling between the two powerful beings. *Note to self. Research gargoyle-dragon relations.*

"Constantine." Roman acknowledged the dragon.

"Montagne." Nikos didn't waver under the gargoyle's regard.

"You are a little out of your territory, Drakon."

Nikos chuckled and his eyes danced with merriment. "New Orleans is neutral territory, Sentinel."

Roman's gaze flicked to Sade before returning to clash with Nikos' amusement. "But she is not."

"Argh!" Sade stepped aside. "I don't have time for who's the biggest dick. I have a plane to catch and a couple of dead magicks to investigate. If you two want to whip 'em out, don't let me stop you but I'll be damned if I stand here and watch. Caleb!"

The werewolf heeled, followed her around the corner then spoke once they were out of sight. "Uhm...Sade? It's not smart to tease a dragon."

"No shit, Sherlock. What was your first clue?"

"Uhm...when you said, *In your dreams* and he said *I'll see you there, darling?*"

She shrugged. "So?"

"So...Nikolas Constantine is a dreamwalker, Sade."

"Well...hell. That gives insomnia a whole new appeal."

136

SOUNDTRACK
THAT OL' BLACK MAGIC

Music is a large part of my creative process and this is especially true with The Penumbra Papers. If you are curious about my play list, here's the soundtrack by chapter by artist and title. All rights to these songs belong to the composers, lyricists, artists, and/or recording companies. I've listed them for informational purposes.

Chapter One: Déjà Vu All Over Again (Inna: Déjà vu)

Chapter Two: Garden of the Dead (Night Wish: Dead Gardens)

Chapter Three: Blood Feud (Lord Huron: I Will Be Back One Day)

Chapter Four: Still of the Night (Kellie Pickler: Someone, Somewhere Tonight)

Chapter Five: Silver Linings (Abney Park: The End of Days)

Chapter Six: Signs (Daughtry: Maybe We're Already Gone)

Chapter Seven: Hands Off (Bon Jovi: Lay Your Hands On Me)

Chapter Eight: Here Be Dragons (OneRepublic: Someone To Save You)

Chapter Nine: One of Those Days (Nickleback: Someday)

Chapter Ten: Decisions (Daughtry: Breakdown)

Chapter Eleven: Caution (Of Monsters and Men: Yellow Light) and (Jason Aldean (with Kelly Clarkson): Don't You Wanna Stay)

Chapter Twelve: Read Between The Lines (Sara Bareilles: Between the Lines)

THE EXCITING URBAN FANTASY
SERIES FROM SILVER JAMES

The Penumbra Papers
Cases from the Shadow's Edge

Penumbra: Etymology: New Latin, from Latin paene almost + umbra shadow

Welcome to the Penumbra Papers. Buried deep within some anonymous warehouse outside of Washington, D.C., there is a wooden box with mystical markings branded into its sides...Oh, wait. Sorry. That's the Ark of the Covenant. My mistake.

The Penumbra Papers actually sit buried in a bottom desk drawer in the office of the Director of the F.B.I. Within its pages, the forces of light and dark dance through shadows which humans had only glimpsed before the dawn of the new age. Since the arrival of the new millennium, all manner of preternatural folks intermingle with humans in ways mysterious and magical or...criminal.

Maybe it was it was the stray star, The Flyer, aligning with Mars. Or the hole in the ozone. Whatever happened in the year 2010, all hell broke loose. Literally. It turned out that there really were monsters under the bed and the things that went bump in the night were bigger and scarier than anyone could imagine.

Vampires. Ghouls. Faeries. Ghosts. Werewolves. Creatures of legend and nightmares. Overnight, reality took on a whole new meaning. And that's where Sade Marquis enters the mix. An FBI agent with an X-Files mentality, she was handpicked to fill a new slot within the Bureau – Preternatural Liaison Officer with the MAGIC Unit. It's Sade's job to deal with all the bad nasties.

The world's best and brightest from every discipline—physics, theology, anthropology, chemistry, to name only a few—all tried to explain the rip in the cosmic curtain. Sade has her own theory. The monsters have been here all along, width:963px; height:1588px;

flying just under the radar of normal perception. They've been masquerading as mundanes—their term for humans. Of course, Sade knows the truth of the matter. Her boss doesn't need to know she was raised by a master vampire or that her pet "dog" shifted into a boy the night of her twelfth birthday. That's Sade's secret. She has a lot of them and she is very, very good at keeping secrets. Which makes her very, very good at her job. And that makes the magicks very, very afraid of her. As they should be...

SEASON OF THE WITCH
Penumbra Papers #1

Sade Marquis. Her best friend turns furry. Her godfather is a master vampire. Her mother was once the mistress of Oberon, King of the Faerie Court.

When the Veil between the mortal and magical realms rips, FBI Special Agent Sade Marquis is in a unique position to head up the newly-formed MAGIC unit. She's the only human who knows exactly what goes bump in the night. When things go to hell in a handbasket and there's magic in the air, Sade is the agent FBI Director George Bailey wants in the trenches. She's savvy, snarky, and sexy but she may have met her match when she's sent to Chicago to investigate the murder of a congressional aide.

Is the vampire, Kristian St. John, guilty as sin? Once a Templar knight, Sinjen now teaches ancient history at the University of Chicago. He must rely on Sade to clear his name and track the real culprit.

Together, they unravel the clues to a mystery that began a thousand years before. If they don't solve the murders of six young women, the whole world—human *and* magick—will suffer the evil consequences.

COMING in 2015
THE DEVIL'S CUT

In the next book in the Penumbra Papers, Caleb Jones is undercover investigating a Mexican drug lord, the death of a

US Border agent, and a couple of missing teenage werewolves. Along the way, he discovers a "devil" has been invoked and he sets out on the trail of the Native American relics needed to set the manitou free in the human world.

At the same time, Colorado Bureau of Investigation technical investigator, Adele Kincaid, is processing the evidence in a series of baffling murders. They all have one thing in common—Native American fetishes. As she works her angle, she bumps into an interesting man, but one who raises her hackles, figuratively. When they are captured by the drug lord, tied up and left in a small plane on a collision course with a mountain, she has to rely on his strange abilities to save them. Hiking through the desert proves an education all its own, and by the time they reach civilization, she's totally smitten, though hurt by his reticence to get involved with her. So what if he turns furry at the drop of a hat? She can live with that. Just so long as they survive the manitou tracking them.

IF YOU ENJOYED THIS BOOK, YOU MAY ALSO ENJOY THE MOONSTRUCK SERIES:

Moonstruck: What happens when a Wolf finds the woman who steals his heart. Blood rushes south and it's a lot like getting hit by a truck.

Warning: When you cross paths with an Alpha Wolf, hot sex, bad words, and violence of the blood and guts kind ensues.

The existence of Wolves has remained a secret for over 200 years. Now, the members of Army Special SciOps Unit 69 are about to be exposed. They'll do whatever it takes to protect their mates and their children.

Available Now in Print and Digital
Moonstruck: Secrets

Coming soon –
Two New Series set in the world of Moonstruck

Nightriders MC
Night Shift – Book 1

Hard Target
Double Cross – Book 1

Also Coming in 2015:

The Full-length Moonstruck Novels
Moonstruck: Secrets
Moonstruck: Lies
Moonstruck: Betrayal
Moonstruck: Retribution

Penumbra Papers
The Devil's Cut

Still Available – the original digital novellas in

MOONSTRUCK
The Award-winning Series

BOOK LIST BY SERIES

Moonstruck:
*Blood Moon – Book 1
*Bad Moon – Book 2
*Hunter's Moon – Book 3
*Wolf Moon – Book 4
*Bride's Moon – Book 5
*Rogue Moon – Book 6
*Christmas Moon – A Moonstruck Novella (#7)
*Blue Moon – Book 8
*Moon Shot – Book 9
*A Moonstruck/Hard Target Crossover Novel
Moonstruck: Secrets – Book 10

Penumbra Papers:
That Ol' Black Magic
Season of the Witch

Mystery Novella:
*Café Midnight

From Harlequin Desire
Red Dirt Royalty
Cowgirls Don't Cry
The Cowgirl's Little Secret

From the Wild Rose Press:
Faerie Fate
Faerie Fire
Faerie Fool
*Faerie Reign
(Digital boxed set of first three books at a special price)
*Faerie Faith (Twelve Brides of Christmas)

Class of '85 Reunion Series:
*Fairy Tales Can Come True
*Promises, Promises

Dearly Beloved Series:
*Best Laid Plans

*Available in Digital Formats Only

ABOUT THE AUTHOR

Silver likes walking cn the wild side and coffee. Okay. She loves coffee. LOTS of coffee. Warning: Her Muse, Iffy, runs with scissors and can be quite dangerous. An award-winning author, she's been a military officer's wife, mother, state appellate court marshal, airport rescue firefighter and forensic fire photographer, crime analyst, technical crime scene investigator, and writer of magic and mystery. Now retired from the "real world," she lives in Oklahoma and spends her days at the computer with two Newfoundland dogs, the cat who rules them all, and myriad characters all clamoring for attention. She writes dark urban fantasy thrillers, time travel romance, and sexy contemporary romance.

To find out more about Silver and her books, visit her website: www.silverjames.com. She loves to connect with readers on Facebook (Silver James, Author) and Twitter (@SilverJames_).